Invaded Dreams

Invaded Dreams

by
J.R.P. Morse

Invaded Dreams

Cover and interior design by Bethany Press International.
Printed by Bethany Press International

ISBN: 978-0-578-02844-6

Scripture quotations are taken from the Holy Bible, New Living Translation, copyright © 1996, 2004, 2007. Used by permission of Tyndale House Publishers Inc. Carol Stream, Illinois 60188. All rights reserved.

"*Invaded Dreams* is an engaging story set on the Kenya coast. Readers will enjoy the blend of romance and religion as Ellen and Raheem meet and struggle to understand each other and the core of their beliefs."

Shel Arensen
Author of *Dust of Africa* and the *Rugendo Rhino* series

In memory of Roshan

1   Terrorist

Sunday, September 10th

The steward pulled and pushed on the lever, locking the door of the airplane while a flight attendant welcomed the last passenger—a tall, well-built, Arab-looking man.

Ellen's attention—or could it be her suspicion?—focused on him. Shifting a small bag and black jacket to free his right hand, he greeted the attendant with a handshake.

A handshake, observed Ellen. *He's probably not American. Maybe he's from India?*

With his fingers, the man brushed thick, black hair off his sweaty forehead.

He's been running and is catching his breath. Or is he nervous about something?

Ellen Johnson, seated in row twelve, was flying back home to Mombasa, Kenya, after a visit with her parents in Dallas, Texas. The Johnsons had taught in Mombasa for thirty years and had now retired to the United States. Ellen had loved growing up in Africa. After her university studies in the U.S., she returned to work in the same city in Africa.

Even though the coastal port city of Mombasa blended many races in a peaceful mix, Ellen's blonde hair and white skin stood out among her African and Indian friends. She didn't mind being different—even impulsively different.

Ellen covered a yawn with the back of her hand. Her itinerary included four flights and two long layovers. Finally, on her third flight,

London to Nairobi, the seat next to her was empty. If it weren't for take-off, she'd be curled up and asleep.

The man looked up the aisle without even glancing at his boarding pass. He spotted the empty seat beside Ellen and moved toward it.

"Please, God, send him away," she prayed silently.

Muttering to himself, he rearranged the luggage in the overhead bin above her. Without tipping the small bag, he carefully wedged it into the space. He pulled the compartment lid down. It popped back up.

What's in that little black bag? Ellen wondered. Of course he had gone through security, yet she imagined the bag had... *He handles it like glass.*

Ellen noted irritation on his face. An attendant offered to close the bin. He sighed and looked down at Ellen. His attractive eyes startled her.

"Hello." He nodded. "I hate being late. Running through an airport attracts security."

"You can relax now." She said it more to convince herself than him. "Welcome."

His knees dug into the seat in front of him as his body folded into the small space. He nodded a smile at Ellen as if to say, 'you're pleasant'. Extending his hand, he introduced himself. "I'm Raheem."

She shook it and tried not to notice the strong muscles in his tan arms.

"I'm Ellen."

His white teeth contrasted with the caramel-colored, tea-stained teeth of most of her Indian friends. She decided to be friendly. "So, what made you late?"

"I overslept." He folded his jacket neatly and looked for a place to store it.

"Here, I have room," Ellen said on impulse. She placed the jacket under the seat in front of her.

"Usually people don't talk to me while on planes. They think I'm a terrorist." He winked a smile. "Thanks for being friendly." Thick black lashes rimmed kind green eyes.

Still trying to persuade herself, she said, "I don't think terrorists shake hands with women." She changed the subject. "What do you do?"

"I just finished being a student. I'm in the medical field, at least I hope—after eight years of sleepless study. I'm on my way home."

"And where is that?"

"Mombasa. I'm a Kenyan Asian."

Ellen relaxed. The Johnsons knew plenty of families in Mombasa. *I'm sure I know someone who has met this man, unless he's...* "So, you're going to be a doctor? Will you work at Mombasa Hospital or Coast General, or maybe The Aga Khan or Pandya Hospital?"

"You know Mombasa?"

"Yeah, it's my home too."

"You—live there?"

"All my life."

"I haven't seen you before." He kept looking at her.

"Well," Ellen thought for a second, "Mombasa has over a million and a half people in it. And you've been gone how many years?"

"Eight." He fixed his green eyes on hers.

"Chances are you wouldn't have seen me." She looked away.

"Very few pretty, blue-eyed, blonde Americans live there. You people sort of stand out. I thought I knew most of the Americans in Mombasa. How many years have you lived there?"

"I was born at the Aga Khan Hospital nearly twenty-six years ago. I schooled at Coast Academy, high schooled in Nairobi, went to college in Texas and returned to work—"

She stopped. She was giving too much information to this stranger. "What about you?"

"There's not much." He looked down at his hands. They were the skilled hands of a doctor, not rough like a mechanic's or a construction worker's. "We live in a traditional home in Old Town. I'm an only child. A year ago my dad died."

"I'm sorry," she folded her hands. "You must miss him."

"We were close." He took a deep breath. "My dad ran several businesses and owned rental buildings. He faithfully attended our mosque." He paused remembering with a sad smile. "He was very religious."

"Are you like him?" Ellen said.

"I run businesses and own properties too, but when I decided to join the medical field my dad didn't like it. He told me more than once that caring too much, having too much concern for other people, was my weakness."

Ellen understood. As a child she played at an orphanage two buildings from her home. Her mother insisted she finish her homework before playing with the orphans. She argued that multiplication tables were not as important as loving castaway children.

"Are you religious?" Ellen asked.

"I was before I left home." He looked at Ellen. "My mother and my friend, Ali, will insist I attend the mosque when I get home. Are you religious?"

"No, but I believe in God and have a personal friendship with him."

"A personal friendship? A pretty lady like you must be his favorite daughter."

"I am." She nodded and smiled.

"Wow, the number-one daughter of God."

"You could be the number-one son of God."

Ellen said this without thinking and his reply was unexpected.

"I've heard Christians say that's who Jesus is."

"Jesus is not that kind of son. Jesus is God himself in human form."

"Really!" He rubbed his chin. "If God is God, he can't be a human. The two don't mix."

"Why not? God created everything, has all power, can do anything, even things we don't understand. Why can't he be all God and all human to give..." Ellen paused, "a great gift to those he loves?"

Raheem thought for a minute. "Five minutes on a plane and we're deep in religious talk."

"Okay, I'll change the subject. How is your mom? I mean, since your dad died?"

"She's depressed. Depressed mothers from my Indian community are difficult." He shook his head. "She emails and calls me everyday, chattering and worrying constantly."

"Has it been eight years since you lived with her?"

"I flew home for a few summers, but yes, it's been a long time." He sighed and pressed the back of his neck with one hand.

"From what I know about Indian families," Ellen smiled with flirty eyes, "your mother has arranged a suitable girl for you."

"Yes, and I will marry only the girl I love." He mimicked the flirty smile back at her.

Ellen's heart skipped a beat and her face flushed. With a slow deep breath she steadied her reaction.

Careful, it's been a long time since you felt that kind of a rush and he's a stranger—maybe even a terrorist.

She rubbed her hot face. "I predict a generation clash—a fight with your mom. She will say…" Ellen hesitated. "I'm sorry, but I forgot your name."

"Raheem, Raheem Ashkar."

"She will say, 'Raheem, meddy her! I go to all d' trouble of arranging with d' pe-dents. Now you meddy her or I kick you out of d' house.'"

He laughed. "How do you know my mom can't say her 'r's'?"

The plane gained speed for take-off and Raheem looked irritated again. "No matter how many times I fly, I dislike take-off." From his shirt pocket he grasped a string of light green prayer beads and closed his eyes.

"We're safer here than in a car."

"So I've heard. I just don't like the loudness and the feel of pressure."

The ninety-nine names of Allah won't take away the sound or the feel, she thought.

He fingered one bead at a time as he whispered the names of Allah. Thirty-three beads were on the string. To get through all the ninety-nine names he'd finger the string three times.

"Can you say the names in English so I can hear them?"

"I'm afraid I only know them in Arabic."

Ellen wondered if he understood Arabic but didn't ask. Many of her Muslim friends didn't know Arabic and therefore didn't understand the meaning of the words they recited. It might hurt his pride to admit he recited words he didn't understand, especially being a doctor.

The plane leveled, and the beads went back in his pocket.

"Raheem, if I ask God to help me not be afraid, he helps me." *It beats counting beads.*

"I believe there is only one God and that is Allah."

"If you pray to Allah and say 'Help me not be afraid,' could he, at that moment, make you unafraid?"

The flight attendant handed them packets of tiny crackers and offered them a beverage. They both ordered coffee.

"I can't know Allah's mind or his will."

"No, no one can know that." She paused. "I believe there is only one God too. He's the one who created us."

"Then, we believe in the same God." He smiled. His skilled hands poured crackers out of the packet onto the open napkin like a pharmacist counting tablets.

Ellen took a small bag of peanuts out of her purse and continued, "I believe Creator God personally loves each human he made."

"You said that. You said we could all be his number one child, but I don't think Allah is that personal."

Ellen considered what to say as she rubbed off the red peanut skins.

"I see you don't eat the red skins," he observed.

"I don't like things that tickle my throat. I have asthma and the feeling of swelling in my throat makes me uncomfortable."

"Does that mean you can't eat hot chili foods—Indian cuisine?"

"I love Indian dishes—*biriyani, mughali, dosas*—as long as they're mild."

He had a mischievous look on his face. "As a doctor, I have just what you need." He stood up and carefully took down the little bag.

That bag! Ellen tensed. *I don't need anything from that little bag.*

"I'm teasing. Actually, I'm going to mix my favorite drink, coffee and yogurt." Out of the bag he took a container of yogurt.

Ellen sighed.

After Raheem stirred a big scoop into his coffee he said, "In my culture it's rude to eat in front of someone. Here try it." He handed the yogurt to her. Feeling a little apprehensive, she slowly mixed in a spoonful.

"Most of my Indian friends drink chai, the sweet milky tea," Ellen said.

"After living in the States, I'm not pure Indian. This is my own invention and yogurt calms my stomach. I worked so hard as a med student that I think I got ulcers. Now you know my weakness."

"And you know mine—asthma."

"Have you eaten at Shehnai?" asked Raheem. "It's the best Indian food in Mombasa."

"Mmm, it's one of my favorite restaurants. I also enjoy the food at Tudor Water Sports on the inlet."

"You haven't tasted anything until you savor a meal of my mom's cooking. She makes perfect mutton pilau. Could I invite you for dinner?"

"You know as well as I do that a single girl is considered reckless with no honor or respect if she goes into a man's home alone...."

"I could invite a group for dinner."

"No."

"No?"

"We are two strangers on a plane. In less than half an hour you ask me to dinner. I'm not ready to go to your house for dinner. Can we change the subject again?"

"Sure, but one more question. Where in Mombasa do you eat out for something quick and tasty?"

"I like the Swahili coconut cuisine at Island Dishes, the one in Old Town."

With his mouth half open Raheem turned to her. "Really! The manager's son, Hatim, is my good friend."

"The manager is my landlord." As soon as she said it she wished she hadn't.

Think before you speak! He will find out where you live!

He's okay. In fact he's fun, and I like him.

You'll regret this.

I'm not falling in love. It takes me years to fall in love.

Then why is your heart pounding?

I'm just overtired.

Raheem asked the flight attendant for a Kenyan newspaper. She handed him *The Daily Nation*. Two articles about the coast appeared on the fifth page.

Ellen noticed them. "In eight years the only thing that's changed in Mombasa is the population. The water pipes are mostly dry, roads fill with pot holes each time it rains, and garbage collection vehicles still need repair. It would be classified a war zone if it weren't for the people. I love the people. Mombasa is the friendliest city I know."

Raheem smiled. "Thank you. That's very kind. I think we're the friendliest people too." He folded up the paper and yawned. "Here, would you like to read? I feel sleepy." He arranged the small white pillow behind his head.

An article caught Ellen's attention, *Drugs Seized by Malindi Police*. Malindi, a tourist town north of Mombasa, was known to harbor Italian mafia. The article mentioned a drug baron named Mr. Ashkar.

Ashkar! Didn't Raheem say his name was Ashkar?

Ellen glanced sideways at him only to find him looking at her. She looked back at the paper. A numb feeling spread over her.

I'm sitting next to a drug dealer.

"May I explain?" asked Raheem. "I am an Ashkar, and sadly I'm related to that man. I am his nephew. He ruined our family name and made life miserable for my father. He still makes it miserable for my mother. Do you want to hear the story?"

Ellen nodded.

"My dad, a religious and good man, loved his dad, my grandfather. As a young boy he would sit at grandfather's desk, writing receipts and balancing books. It was natural for him to inherit the business and the traditional home." Raheem sat up and put the pillow in his lap.

"His younger brother, Abdul, skipped school, hung out with useless people, and was in and out of court. He learned the art of bribing officials and judges, so he isn't afraid of the law." Raheem tapped the newspaper. "Nor does he mind getting himself in the news.

"He joined up with Italian criminals who laundered money in Malindi buying beach cottages. He finally made his million. With the cash, he built a house on the inlet.

"Mindless addicts and dealers slept on his steps. Women and wives moved in and out. His money never lasted. Abdul is cunning and evil, always after more. As you know, my father died a year ago. Dad left his wealth to me. My mom is worried that Uncle Abdul will swindle it from me."

He looked at Ellen. "So there you have it."

"He must be a constant stress."

"I'm determined to be his opposite. He lives to please himself. I live my life to help others. That's why I became a doctor." He placed the pillow back behind his head. "I'm too tired to think about him." He closed his eyes.

Since Kenya Airways did not assign seats on the short Nairobi to Mombasa flight, Raheem and Ellen sat together again. The plane landed, and as it taxied into Moi Airport in Mombasa, Raheem leaned close to

Ellen on the armrest between their seats. "Before we get off the plane I have a confession to make." A sly smile lit his eyes. "You left your passport partly sticking out of your purse and I looked at it while you were in the restroom."

"You horrible snoop." Ellen's jaw bit down on her back teeth. "What did you find out about me?" *He better not be a drug baron or terrorist.*

"Your birthday is October first." His eyebrows bobbed twice. "You're much prettier than that passport picture."

Ellen felt anything but pretty. Her blonde, shoulder-length hair was twisted in a knot at the back of her neck. Her tan skin with a sprinkle of freckles felt dirty and clammy. The whites of her blue eyes, red from lack of sleep, were smoldering. Raheem annoyed her.

"If you want to be my friend, then ask before you touch any of my things."

His eyes danced with a teasing sparkle. With his hand on his chest and chin held high, he mimicked a British accent, "I most sincerely apologize. May I ask, my dear lady, if I may assist you in taking down your bag from the overhead bin?"

Ellen was not amused. *What have I done? Is he going to stalk me?*

Mombasa's humidity hit like a wall as Ellen stepped out of the plane. For a moment, it was hard to breathe the thick air. The steep metal steps wobbled as they climbed down.

Walking next to her on the steamy tarmac, Raheem asked, "Is a welcome party here to celebrate your return?" He pointed at the airport building.

"No, I'm expecting a friend who will drive me home. But knowing your culture, the whole extended family will be here to greet you."

"Yes, I dread it. I've traveled for thirty-eight hours, am exhausted, and need a shower." With the palm of his hand, he pushed his hair back. "My hair is sticking to my head. Fifteen people will need embracing. I have to smile and perform my cultural greetings."

"You look fine." She stopped walking. "May I say good-bye here? Those relatives scare me." She moved her bag to her left hand. "Raheem, I enjoyed sitting by you. I wish you God's peace and truth—"

"Wait. I can't say good-bye." He shifted his feet. "Mombasa is a huge city and we didn't meet in the past twenty-six years. The thought of not meeting you again is...let's...." He stumbled over his words.

"Your birthday is October first. I'll be at Island Dishes for coconut cuisine at seven o'clock sharp." He smiled with one eyebrow up. "Celebrate with me?"

"Ahh," Ellen stammered. "Maybe I shouldn't—"

Raheem interrupted, "Just come." With a pleased grin on his face, he held out his hand. She shook it.

"Thanks for being yourself," he said.

"Thanks for not being a terrorist." His green eyes shot a look into her eyes and straight to her heart. She would never forget him. Her hand was still in his—trembling. She let go.

"See you," he said.

He is a terrorist and has no right attacking my heart. I don't even know him. He's an Ashkar drug dealer! Those eyes...they'll invade my dreams, my daydreams, my random thoughts...but he cares about people...and has given his life to heal people!

2   **Ellen**

Friday morning, September 29ᵗʰ

Ellen finished setting breakfast for three on a card table on the roof patio. At the walled edge, she looked across Mombasa. Below, like a messy blanket quilted in browns, grays, and reds, the roofs shaped the top of the city. Rusty corrugated metal, red slanting rows of tile, and flat chipped plaster covered the buildings.

A fascinating mix of people lived in those buildings: coastal Bantu Africans, upcountry Kenyans, the Swahili people group, Arabs in checkered turbans, and Indians from their many communities dressed in bright saris or Punjabi outfits.

On the street below, a man with a wooden cart filled with fruit looked up at apartment windows and yelled, "*matunda*"—fruit in Swahili. A maid on the third floor dropped a woven basket on a rope for him to fill.

A tall, well-built Indian man stopped and picked through the oranges on the cart. He combed his fingers through his hair.

Is it him?

Ellen unlocked the security gate and ran downstairs. She needed bananas.

As she ran up to the cart, the tall Indian was walking away. Once again she was mistaken.

The fruit vender knew Ellen well. He was from the coastal Swahili tribe and wore his traditional plaid long-sleeved shirt and a dull-colored striped cloth called a *kikoi* wound tight at his waist.

The Swahili were descendents of Arab-Bantu marriages from slave days and the oldest people group living in Mombasa. Their women covered themselves head-to-toe in black robes called *buibuis*.

The vender picked out three nice bananas for Ellen's ten shillings.

At seven the street filled with school kids in uniforms and backpacks. Maids walked with the little ones.

Most maids were coastal Bantu Kenyans wrapped in bright two-piece matching cloths, like tablecloths with borders.

Coastal Bantu men dressed in striped *kikois* like the Swahili men. These Kenyans were a total contrast to upcountry Kenyans who wore ironed suits and ties—classic western outfits.

This mix created Mombasa. Different races and tribes lived side-by-side—some even in the same buildings—and they generated Mombasa's friendly atmosphere. Each had their own beliefs: Muslim, Hindu, Christian, and African traditional religions.

As Ellen returned to her building, someone called to her. "Hey, Ellen, wait up."

Priscilla, nicknamed Zillah, tucked an extension braid back in her hair band as she looked both ways and cautiously crossed the street. She didn't take chances. Her long thin braids, straight-cut jeans, and dark pink top made her look tall.

"Welcome," Ellen said. "Glad you came early. How's your family?"

They climbed the steps and Ellen unlocked the gate.

"They're eating a dull Kikuyu breakfast while I feast at your rooftop flat. I love breakfast up here."

Zillah's family came from the upcountry Kikuyu tribe. Her dad had moved to the coast to work at the port.

A white cloth covered the little card table. Zillah admired the plate of mango slices as Ellen added bananas. She peeked under a yellow-checkered towel covering warm toast in a woven basket. "It's set for a queen."

"Thank you," Ellen said, "It's just simple."

"Why do simple foods look so good up here? You're so lucky to have this place."

Ellen rented a two-room apartment with a rooftop patio in downtown Mombasa. Just below on the third floor, she also rented a four-room apartment where she ran a center for disadvantaged children.

Zillah continued, "Asmina and I are happy you're back, and the kids missed you too."

"You're always kind. It's been three weeks since I returned from visiting my parents and you all act like every day is another welcome party."

"That's because we *did* miss you."

Along the outer stairwell wall, Ellen had created a hanging garden with dozens of flowering plants arranged with the help of an old clothesline. Zillah walked among them. "I hope your garden is well. We did our best to keep your plants watered and alive."

"You guys did great. It's amazing that they bloom in the heat and wind up here."

Ellen motioned Zillah to the other side of the patio. She had arranged large potted plants and chairs next to the low wall at the far corner.

"Come sit over here. It gives a different view of the city."

"Hey, another garden—but why way over here?"

Ellen hesitated. "Well, because…" She couldn't tell her the real reason. "We can see down on two streets."

They settled in comfortable green lawn chairs.

"I called Asmina earlier. She's on her way. I asked her to stop at the Post Office. She has the key to my box."

Below cars hooted as people dodged in and out of traffic. Auto-rickshaws, called *tuk-tuks,* revved their little engines loudly. These small, three-wheeled motorbikes had a driver and carried only three people on the back seat. When mosques began their calls to prayer, noise flooded Mombasa's crowded streets.

An ex-mayor, four mayors ago, still kept his hand in city affairs. His goal, whether in office or not, was to clean up Mombasa. He had garbage collected on the main streets, trees and flowers planted in the round-a-bouts and medians, and from time to time had most of the beggars sent home. Mombasa really wasn't a war zone.

The doorbell buzzed. Ellen opened the gate and greeted Asmina. She was from the Indian Kaatchi community.

"You got here fast. How are you today?"

Asmina plopped down in a chair by the table and held her head in her hands. "Too much pressure! School, homework, exams, and now my aunt is on me."

"So what's the problem with your aunt?" Ellen smoothed Asmina's gold head scarf. It matched her long red top, trimmed with gold embroidery, which she wore over jeans.

Asmina's parents had died in a bus accident when she was eight and an aunt raised her. Ellen paid her to manage the kids' center. With the money, Asmina paid for college classes.

Invaded Dreams

"She's serious about an arranged marriage for me," Asmina pouted.

"Tell her you're too young." Zillah took a seat at the table.

Ellen turned to Zillah. "In Mina's Indian community, twenty-one is old. Mina, don't most Kaatchi girls get married around sixteen?" Asmina moaned.

"Who does she want you to marry?"

"She knows some guy from our community who was educated in America. He's just come back. Aunty says the guy's mother wants him married right away."

"Have you met him?" Ellen began pouring tea.

"No, thank God...but it's *my* life! Shouldn't I be the one to find who I like? Can you imagine? It's like unmarried girls are sale items. Their mothers shop around and look for the best deals. And get this: I heard six other moms are visiting this guy's mother and asking about him. It's like an auction. She chooses the richest, prettiest, most influential girl who ends up taking care of her more than him. I am so sick of this system."

Trying to cheer up Asmina, Zillah leaned forward with wide eyes. "What makes him such a catch?"

"He's a doctor!"

Ellen stopped pouring tea.

Raheem!

Three weeks had passed since she had met Raheem on the plane. Her work with needy kids was hectic—catching up on financial reports, repairs, buying supplies. But...she had thought of him, had even arranged the patio chairs next to the corner of the roof hoping to see him walk by. How could she forget—those green eyes, the way he tipped his head?

Raheem, not her childhood sweetheart, Rick; nor Norman, the guy she dated in college, but Raheem entered as the main character in those dreams and stories she made up before falling asleep.

In real life he is not for me, she thought. And yet...I'd like to see him.

"A doctor!" Ellen repeated too loudly. "Mina, at least meet him. I'm sure he's way handsome."

"Do you want me to marry a man who doesn't believe the way I do?" Asmina moped.

14

"No, no. You will marry a man who knows and loves Jesus." She finished pouring tea and sat down. "I'll bet Mister Doctor is ugly with three chins and hair all over his body," she teased.

Zillah laughed and joined in, "He overeats, is never home, and hates women."

"Life is so depressing," Asmina whimpered. "Why do guys with decent qualifications end up the pokerfaced deadpans?"

"Cheer up." Zillah patted her hand. "God has a perfect man for you, Mina."

"Yes, he does." Ellen bit her lower lip. "God can do anything, so what if—just what *if* Mister Doctor becomes that right guy? Let's pray for him. Maybe in America he heard about Jesus—"

"Ellen, I will marry the man I love. Pleeease, no arranged marriage for me! Oh, I almost forgot." Asmina reached for her bag and handed Ellen four letters. Three were from Norman.

"Oooo, Zillah, look what she got." She spread the letters out on the table. "Norman Gilberts." Asmina was teasing now. "Tell us about Norm babe!"

"Three letters in one week, that's serious," Zillah raised her eyebrows. "What's he like?"

"I wonder how many emails he sends in one day," Asmina drummed her fingers as if keyboarding.

"You'll meet him and see for yourselves," said Ellen.

"Come on, what does he look like?"

"Well, he looks like me, except he's a guy, blond hair and blue eyes, Dutch."

"What does he do? What does he want in life?" Zillah asked.

"He loves God, is a youth pastor, and grows roses."

"Oooo, I'll bet he gave you red roses." With an extra wide smile, Asmina nodded her head.

"I admit it, yes, and he even got me into growing plants."

"You guys are so alike. Is he impulsive like you?" Zillah reached over and squeezed Ellen's arm. "I love that about you."

"No, he plans everything out. In that trait we're opposites."

"How did you meet him?"

"Well, we worshipped in the same church this past summer. We attended the same classes at college, two years ago. We just met."

"I thought you liked Rick," Asmina frowned, "that guy from Congo."

"I've known Rick all my life. Sometimes I do like him but he's…he has lots of girlfriends."

Ellen had grown up with Rick in Mombasa. Now he worked in a gold and gems business in Congo. He had sent Ellen an e-mail the week before asking her to meet him halfway, in Uganda.

"I remember he looked really rugged," Asmina said.

Ellen decided they needed to get to work. "It's time to get downstairs and clean up before the kids come."

Zillah smiled at Mina. "She must like him. She's changing the subject."

"Maybe she likes both Rick and Norm," Asmina teased.

Maybe you don't know who I like.

The day before, little kids had scattered books all over the floor of the center. The kitchen sink overflowed with dirty dishes. Teenagers had come for dinner and emptied the water tank. Ellen flipped the switch and a pump hummed on the ground floor, pumping water to a tank on the roof.

Mombasa city water drizzled for half an hour through the pipes twice a week. Most residents bought their water from tanker trucks that hauled it from outside the city. It amazed Ellen how a city of a million-and-a-half people survived and why the government did nothing to improve the water supply.

Still, I wouldn't want to leave Mombasa for anything.

"Hey, look." Asmina pointed to the calendar. "Sunday is October first, your birthday!"

"Let's celebrate and take Ellen out for dinner." Zillah suggested.

Ellen's thoughts flashed back to Raheem's words, 'I will be at Island Dishes, seven sharp. Celebrate with me?' She remembered his smile and those kind expressive eyes. *Would he be there? Do I dare meet him? Maybe he forgot October first.*

Zillah and Mina looked at Ellen staring at the pump switch on the wall.

Maybe he's forgotten me. I should forget him—now!

"Earth to Ellen," Mina sang.

"Sorry." Ellen shook her head. "Dinner? Yes, if it's quick and tasty."

"Dreaming about Norman?" Mina kept teasing, "or is it Rick?"

"You deserve a special celebration." Zillah kindly touched her arm.

"I'd like the Swahili coconut cooking at Island Dishes. It's special because...you guys don't have a lot of money and you can afford to take me there."

3   Raheem

Sunday, October 1ˢᵗ

Ellen knew she shouldn't meet Raheem again. A friendship with him would fuel chaos in her emotions. She begged Zillah and Asmina to change their plan but, for some reason, they insisted on going to Island Dishes. Well, if he showed up she'd introduce him to Asmina.

At seven sharp, the girls walked into Island Dishes. Raheem sat at a table facing the door and his eyes drew Ellen's like a magnet. A glow totally disconnected from her brain spread across her face.

This is a mistake. I'm such a fool.

The only empty table happened to be next to his. She couldn't help but notice that he watched her. After they were seated, he stood and came over. With his hands flat on the table, he leaned forward. "I understand someone has a birthday today." His warm smile reflected the same feeling Ellen was trying not to show. "May I join your table?" He shook hands with each girl. "I'm Raheem."

Asmina's big brown eyes stared without blinking. Her mouth hung part way open. Zillah glanced from Ellen to Raheem and back to Ellen with confusion. Ellen gave him a quick look. "You're welcome." She could hardly breathe.

"Before I join you I need to wash my hands. Excuse me." He turned and walked to the sink at the far wall.

"That's…that's him!" Asmina squealed in a whisper. "My Aunt showed me a photo of him." She held her hand to her forehead. "The doctor—Raheem! He is…he's amazing." She let out a big breath. "I'm suddenly interested."

"I hope you're joking," Zillah warned.

"I hope he's saved," Asmina whispered. "How does he know it's your birthday?"

"Oh, no! Look." Zillah bit her lower lip. "Raheem is talking with the manager's son. I confess. Yesterday I asked the manager to bake a special birthday cake, one from an American recipe. I think Raheem…" she finished her sentence slowly, "I think Raheem was here listening to us."

A sigh escaped Ellen. She looked over at him.

What was he saying to Hatim, her landlord's son? He couldn't be that bad. He had been fun and polite on the plane.

He remembered my birthday. He's here—here to see me!

She turned to the girls. "If we get to know him, and if he's not so bad, he'd be a good friend and—"

"The poor orphan girl marries the rich doctor," finished Mina.

Zillah frowned at Asmina. "How can you talk like that?"

"Zillah, look at him!"

"I did look at him. He looks good and he knows it."

"Okay, I'm dreaming." Mina rubbed her cheeks. "But imagine…."

"You can't be serious." Zillah's brow puckered.

"My aunt would be so happy."

Yes, Ellen thought, *a happy aunty, a happy Mina, and a rich man married off. I'd be free from his pursuit, and free from these wild dreams. If only…but he's a Muslim.*

Before Zillah expressed more disapproval, Raheem towered over them with Hatim and a waiter at his side. They balanced two trays crammed with little bowls, a bit of every dish the restaurant offered. The table had no room for elbows. "I guess I over did it?"

"Anyway, let's enjoy a birthday feast." He smiled at Ellen.

Hatim greeted Ellen and her friends. He wished Ellen a happy birthday, and with a big smile he returned to the cashier's counter.

Raheem politely passed food to each girl. Beans, cassava, cooking bananas, chicken, and fish were cooked the traditional Swahili way in coconut milk and spices.

"I love this coconut sauce. The Swahili have the best flavor," Ellen said.

"Except for some Indian dishes," corrected Raheem with a wink at Asmina.

Mina, awestruck, nodded in agreement.

Raheem cut pieces of chicken *tikka* and divided *mishkaki*, beef cubes stuck onto a wooden stick then cooked over charcoal.

"I don't know your names." Raheem looked at the two girls.

"I'm Zillah."

"Zillah. I like that."

"It's short for Priscilla, not Godzilla." Ellen blurted out. They laughed.

Raheem turned to Asmina.

"I'm Mina, Asmina Sodha."

"Doesn't my mother know your aunt?" Raheem asked.

"Yes, they do, ah, quite well—I think." Mina turned her bangles around on her arm.

Raheem sliced a Mombasa pizza, or *mkate mayai* as the Swahili called it, a thick omelet filled with ground beef.

Zillah, still skeptical about Raheem, asked, "Where do you work?"

"I'm jobless, like so many out there." He waved toward the street. Zillah glanced at Ellen with an I-told-you-so look.

"And what do you do?" he smiled at Zillah.

"Ellen runs a center for poor kids. Mina and I work with her."

"I admire that," Raheem signaled with thumbs up. "I've devoted my life to serving people as well. I applied for a job at a hospital."

Ellen kept quiet. He hadn't let on that they had already met. She didn't want the girls to know.

Near the end of the meal Asmina's cell phone buzzed. "Oh, that's my aunt. I must go home."

Zillah also said her parents wanted her home by eight-thirty. Then she remembered, "We forgot the birthday cake. It's in the kitchen."

Raheem's face brightened. "What a good excuse to get together tomorrow. Besides, we've eaten too much to fit in any cake tonight."

Ellen noticed Raheem had eaten very little.

"Tomorrow, here, at the same time?" with eyebrows high he nodded at each girl. "Yes?"

Asmina returned a nod.

"Let me call a taxi." He jumped up. "Ellen, I'll walk you home since you live just around the corner." He ran out the door waving for a taxi.

The girls stared at each other. "Are we coming back tomorrow?" said Asmina.

"Should we?" said Ellen.

"Sure, it'll be fun, with delicious cake and fine-looking company." Mina tried not to smile too big.

"How does he know where you live?" asked Zillah, "This guy is too…"

"Know-it-all," finished Ellen.

"Will you be safe?" Zillah insisted.

"You mean walking with Dr. Raheem?" Mina sighed. "I wish he'd walk with me."

"Mina," Zillah shook her head. "Think. Alone at night with a stranger!"

Raheem had run back in and heard part of the conversation. He smiled at Asmina then turned to Ellen. "I'm sorry. I should have *asked* properly." He stood tall, his heels together and a hand spread across his chest. He put on his British accent. "May I escort you home?"

"I accept your kind offer." She mimicked back.

Everyone laughed except Zillah.

Ellen whispered to Zillah, "He's walking me less than two blocks. I'll be okay."

Outside, Raheem helped the girls into the taxi and paid the driver. As they drove off, he turned to Ellen. "Let's walk the long way, down by Fort Jesus. It's lit up for the Sound and Light Show. We can watch the tourists."

They sat on a low wall near the fort's parking lot and faced the Portuguese sixteenth-century stone-and-mortar fort. Gold-colored spotlights lit the massive walls. Actors dressed as Arabs in colorful robes and turbans, with wide-curved Arabian knives hanging from their belts, stood on guard between the cannons at the fort's gate. Six actors held torches lit with yellow burning flames. Like a drama playing out, tourists ambled into the light between the torches and cannons, then up the ramp and through the heavy studded black doors of Fort Jesus.

"Have you been to the Sound and Light Show?" Raheem spoke first.

"No, but I heard it's an awesome evening."

"Then let's go—next weekend."

Ellen looked away. *That would be romantic,* she thought.

"But maybe…" She looked back at him. "I think we should get to know each other before we set ourselves up for a romantic evening."

"You're a cautious girl and wise. I agree—about being friends first."

The last of a tour group disappeared into the fort. The night settled into silence around them.

"As just a friend, I'd like to get you a little birthday gift. What color do you like?"

"I like green, but I don't think you should get me a gift."

"A gift won't spoil you. What kind of green do you like?"

"I like the greens of forest branches with gold sunlight shining on leaves."

"What do you have that's green?"

"My sofa set and chairs are forest green. But Raheem, I don't accept gifts from guys."

"A gift from me won't hurt you."

A loudspeaker crackled above them. The call to prayer began. It sounded like the voice came out of Fort Jesus as it echoed off the thick walls. It blasted from a mosque two blocks away.

"Green is the color we use in our mosques. It is Allah's color," continued Raheem.

"I think it is God's color too. Once I knelt by a green sofa to pray with my grandmother. She said if I accepted God's forgiveness, through Jesus, he'd deepen my love and knowledge of himself. I'd grow in my love for him like a strong, green tree grows with deep roots."

"Your passion for God amazes me." He looked at her. "Do you want to know *my* favorite color?"

"Tell me."

"Blue. I love sapphires and the deep shades they reflect when they move this way and that. Things that are blue tell stories like the sea and the sky. Blue is the color of the soul, deep, full of feeling; it sparkles." He gazed straight into her eyes.

My eyes are blue. He's talking about me!

"Dear God, help me. Please keep us just friends."

His eyes are a stunning green. Oh, I love green.

Ellen jumped off the wall.

Raheem grabbed her hand. "Don't leave—yet."

She turned and faced him. "Just friends, okay?"

He let go of her hand. "Yes, we are just friends. Forgive me."

She sat on the wall again. "I'm guessing you watch a lot of Bolly-wood movies."

He laughed.

"If you do watch them," Ellen smiled, "then I forgive your romantic gestures."

"Do you think you understand me and my feelings because of Indian movies?"

"If I think that, it wouldn't be fair, would it?"

Raheem didn't answer.

"I'll be fair." Ellen confessed. "I watch Indian movies and like some of them."

"You do?" He raised an eyebrow. "So, do you think we Indian young men long for a hard-to-get, gorgeous, perfect girl?"

"Yes. And we girls long for a man who loves with a perfect love."

Raheem shook his head. "In real life there is no perfect girl, man, or love. Why do we lie to ourselves?"

"I think there is a perfect love, and God put that longing in us so we'd look for it."

"A perfect love?"

"It's a redeeming love."

"A what?"

"A redeeming love is given by God because he's the only one who loves perfectly."

"Ellen, you're talking—deep."

"It's like a man who loves his wife and he gives her everything she needs. Yet she's untrue to him. He still loves her and longs for her devotion to him. He can't stop loving her. She's valuable to him. He'll give his life for her."

"Is that what God does?"

"Yes, God gave his life for us because we have all been untrue to him. That's redeeming love."

"There's no man who would love a wife like that."

"But there are men who ask God for his perfect love. That's what I'm looking for, not a perfect man."

"Most of the girls in my community have little say in who they marry."

"Yes. I know. But I've heard marriages work in your community if kind and good parents match the couple. Right?"

"I will marry only the girl I love. Then I'll do my best to be a good husband."

"God will help you."

"How do you know?"

"Because I'll pray that you seek God and that you find him."

A smile slowly spread across Raheem's face. "You must like me...a little."

"It's time for me to go home." Ellen stood up and turned in the direction of her street. She didn't want him to see her uncontrolled smile.

Raheem walked beside her, laughing softly. "You're fun to tease."

The moment was interrupted. "Raheem!" Two men in white robes and prayer caps approached them. "Hey, man, where were you tonight? We missed you at prayers."

The men shook hands and kept walking along with Raheem and Ellen.

"Who's your friend? Is she visiting Kenya?"

"Ellen has lived here nearly all her life," Raheem informed them. He turned to Ellen and motioned to the taller man. "Ali is our honored Imam, our mosque leader, and my friend."

Ali's habit was not to shake hands with women. He didn't extend his hand to Ellen.

She wondered if Allah would forgive Raheem who had skipped prayers to be with a non-Muslim woman.

"And this is my good friend Naushad."

Naushad reached over and shook Ellen's hand. "What was your name?" he asked.

"Ellen Johnson. My father taught at Mombasa High School."

"I know him! My father had a computer repair shop and did the repairs for the computer lab. Your dad is a tall guy with hair the color—the same color as yours and he wore a baseball cap."

"That's him."

"I think we've met a long time ago. Where did you go to school?"

"I attended Coast Academy from standard one to standard eight. Then I went to—"

"Coast Academy!" Ali interrupted and took a good look at Ellen. "I remember you. At lunchtime you traded your hamburgers for my chicken *tikka*. Remember?"

"You're that skinny kid, Ali? Yes, I remember. You were always nice to me."

Ali extended both hands. "Ellen, you have changed!"

Ali turned to Raheem. "How did you meet my classmate?"

"On the plane three weeks ago. Today is her twenty-sixth birthday."

"Hey, you look eighteen!" Ali said. "If you were in our community, you'd be married and have a house full of kids."

Ellen laughed. "I may not be married yet, but I do have a house full of kids; at least some of the time." She described her work at the children's center.

They reached Ellen's building.

"I hope we meet again," she said, as she opened the gate.

"I can't believe it's you, Ellen," Ali shook his head.

She turned to Raheem. "Thanks for escorting me. I'm going to leave you with your friends. Goodnight."

Raheem gave her hand two squeezes. His eyes danced with pleasure. "See you tomorrow," he whispered.

Ellen climbed the stairs to her apartment. Her right hand extended frozen in a hand-shake position. She could feel the squeezes. *I can't let that happen again.* And now, how would she act around Raheem?

A Muslim man is courting me!

She never dreamed it would happen to her.

4

The Curse

Monday, October 2nd

At three-thirty the doorbell to the kids' center buzzed. Inside, Zillah and Ellen helped several boys with schoolwork and Asmina played a game of memory cards with three five-year-old kids on the carpet. Ellen answered the door.

I knew he'd stalk me.

"Hi, Raheem."

"Am I disturbing you?"

"Come in."

"Oh no, I'll just be a second." He stopped in the doorway and looked into the room over her shoulder. "I'm disturbing your work."

Ellen felt everyone behind her watching.

"There's a change of plans. My mother insists we bring the cake to our home and have a party with her this evening."

"No, I can't go to your house," Ellen whispered.

"It's not a date," he answered softly.

"I'll go back to Island Dishes."

"Being friends is all it is."

Ellen noticed he looked different, thin and pale.

"Naushad, Ali, and Hatim want to be your friends too," Raheem reasoned.

Two young boys came up behind Ellen. One reached for her hand and leaned against her arm. Raheem winked at the boy and asked to see the math book he held. He turned the book over and nodded a knowing smiled at the back cover then handed the book back.

Ellen leaned down and hugged each boy. "I'll be right with you. Go back to the table and try the next problem." She knew the other kids would want to talk with Raheem.

"Okay, we'll go," she whispered. "But please don't ask me to your house again—even with friends." His eyes held her gaze like a trap. *Why do I let him attack my heart with just a glance?*

That evening Raheem and Naushad walked the three girls to Island Dishes to collect the cake. Ali had a mosque function and couldn't come. Hatim joined the group as they left Island Dishes for Raheem's house. As was the custom, the guys walked ahead and the girls followed in their group.

After fifteen minutes, Raheem gestured to a white building. "Welcome to my humble home."

It was not what Ellen expected. Like a child's drawing, one wooden door stood in the center of a big, white-washed wall with two little square windows on either side.

"My great-grandfather bought the house. It's a traditional Swahili home." As they stepped through the heavy wood door, Ellen noticed vines and leaves delicately carved on the door posts from top to bottom.

"This is beautiful." She peered closer.

"Raheem's great-grandfather carved it," informed Naushad.

"He made this! Now it's more amazing." Ellen rubbed her fingers along the smooth leaves and flowers. *These doorposts belong in a palace.*

Inside the door they removed their shoes and stepped onto a spotless white tile floor. A trace of curry spice and fried pastries filled the air. A wide hallway divided the house in two. "It's a simple house," Raheem explained. "The three rooms on the left are first my room, then the living room, and Mom's bedroom back there." He pointed. "And the three rooms on the right are the guest room, the dining room, and the kitchen."

"I didn't imagine you living in a Swahili house." Ellen took another look around.

I dreamed he lived in a castle, or at least a big, two-story Arab house.

"I have a look-out tower." Raheem teased and pointed up. There was no ceiling. The top part of the corrugated roof was raised higher than the rest of the rafters leaving an open area in all four directions.

"Each room opens into this big hall and hot air is drawn out through the open roof."

"It's much cooler than my house," Zillah agreed.

"The Swahili people have air-conditioned their homes this way for centuries," Naushad explained.

Raheem's mother appeared from the kitchen laden with a tray of finger foods. "Welcome, come, come." She wore a white headscarf and a flowered pastel dress that hung like a barrel on her plump body.

She beckoned the group into the sitting room. "Call me Mama or Mama Raheem." The girls sat on one side of the room and the guys on the other. After setting the tray on a coffee table, she shook hands with each person, pausing to look at Asmina.

Brown furniture filled the sitting room except for a huge, glass cabinet. It was stuffed with ornaments, decorated brass plates with engraved Koran verses, and glass miniatures of mosques with minarets honoring Islam and Mecca.

Mama picked up a plate of fried potato pieces called *bajiahs* and handed them to Hatim. "You like my cooking more than Island Dishes, don't you?" She nudged his shoulder with her elbow.

Little triangle pastries with meat inside called *samosas* were on another plate she handed to Ellen.

"*Samosas* are my favorite. Did you make these?" Ellen reached for a piece.

"She must cook everything fresh," Raheem answered.

"You mean she makes her own *chevda*?" Zillah asked in amazement. *Chevda,* or *chevdro* as some call it, is a mix of yellow saffron, dried rice, peas, lentils and peanuts.

"Take more. Take a big plateful." Mama offered more food to Asmina who had only a tiny bit on her plate. Ellen noticed Mama gave Raheem a small glass of milk. He didn't eat the food.

A tapestry hung above the sofa, woven in red and gold. It pictured the Kaaba, the sacred house in Mecca, with thousands of people walking around it. On another wall, near the ceiling, hung a large photo of the Great Mosque lit up at night. Ellen knew about these places in Mecca. Many of her friends had made the hajj or pilgrimage. "Have you been to Mecca?" Ellen asked Raheem.

He carefully removed the decorated birthday cake from its box. "No, but my parents went."

"We are arranging for him to go next year," Mama said. "It is a great honor for our family."

"I have a question about hajj. When a person completes the pilgrimage, are his sins forgiven so Allah will accept him?"

"While in Mecca," Naushad explained, "we believe a person is pure and forgiven. If one dies on hajj, he goes to paradise. Those who complete hajj are closer to Allah, but no one knows who Allah will accept into paradise."

A loud knock rattled the door and a tall man stomped into the sitting room. He stopped abruptly, not expecting visitors. He frowned with deep wrinkles at Naushad and Hatim. Then he glared at the girls.

Raheem introduced him. "This is Uncle Abdul." Ellen noticed a deep scar on his neck. Raheem rose and escorted him back outside.

Mama sighed. "He's always that way. Don't mind him. Here, take more *bajiahs*. Eat. More *samosas*?"

Ellen sensed anxiety in Mama's voice.

After nearly an hour, Raheem returned. It was time for Mina and Zillah to go home.

With a look of disgust and frustration, Raheem apologized. "Uncle Abdul is in constant trouble and he threatens me if I don't help him. With all my heart, Ellen, I wanted to celebrate your birthday tonight."

Outside the door, as the group said good-bye to Mama, a fluttering, scratching noise drew their attention to the corrugated roof. An owl had landed on the TV antenna. Mama rushed into the house, upset and disturbed.

"What happened?" asked Ellen.

"The owl brings the curse of death," said Raheem.

"Do you believe that?"

"I suppose I could…. My mother will try to keep the curse away. She'll make a little scarecrow and have it attached to the antenna."

As they walked, Raheem explained. "My community believes in spirits both good and bad. Uncle Abdul has used a spirit to place a curse on me because I inherited the family businesses and he wants them. He says I'll die of cancer like my father did. Others in my extended family say he has the evil-eye because he's jealous of me." Raheem shook his head. "I don't want any part of it."

"I believe there are spirits and spiritual power," said Ellen. "I'm glad God's spirit lives in me. He keeps all other spirits and curses from disturbing me."

"You have strength, Ellen, which I admire."

"It's not my strength."

They stopped at the main road. Zillah and Asmina took a *tuk-tuk* home. Naushad and Hatim left for Island Dishes, and Raheem walked Ellen back to her flat.

"Raheem, you said you don't want any part of the power of spirits. Is it because you don't believe in their power?"

"No, their power is real." His eyes were wide. "And it's scary."

"Yes, it is," agreed Ellen. "In the Koran it talks about the Book. The Book is from God. It says Jesus came and can free us from the power of evil if we accept him."

"Mombasa is known as the city of spirits." Raheem explained. "I don't know of any community here that is free from their power."

"Yes, I've heard that too. Many people here live in fear of evil spirits. I would, too, if it weren't for what God has done for me. Through Jesus, God made a way for me to be free from Satan and all his evil spirits. Plus God gave me his own Spirit who specializes in peace and truth."

They stopped at Ellen's gate.

"Could we continue this conversation another time?" Raheem opened the gate and didn't wait for an answer. "And could Naushad and I visit your kids' center tomorrow afternoon?"

"Tomorrow we help kids with schoolwork and we tutor. Around three o'clock we have story time and then make a craft. After that we play games. It's boring—unless you join in."

"Can we come?" He looked at her with bright eyes.

Ellen looked away.

"Just say yes, and if we aren't helpful, ask us to leave."

She nodded.

"See you at three tomorrow, and I'll bring your birthday gift." He turned to walk away before she could protest.

"Raheem, I'll refuse it," she called after him.

Ellen thought about Raheem's home, his way of life and his mother. Maybe he had lived in America for eight years, but that Swahili home was not a bit American. He and his mom were strong Muslims.

They had nothing in common with Ellen. Getting to know him better had shown her he was not for her. She needed to tell him not to keep seeing her.

The next day Raheem didn't show up. After four days Ellen grew more concerned. She had heard nothing from him. She'd speak with Hatim at Island Dishes.

Saturday, October 7th

About five o'clock on Saturday, as Ellen cleaned and closed up the kids' center, Raheem walked in. Ellen noticed no smile or spark in his eyes. He immediately apologized for not contacting her sooner. A serious problem had taken him time to sort out. "I need you to come with me to a book shop. We must hurry because the shop is about to close. It's on Moi Avenue by the Tusks. We'll be back in thirty minutes. Can Zillah and Mina close up here?"

Raheem wore that irritated look, that same look Ellen remembered when she first saw him getting on the airplane. Without hesitating, she agreed to go with him.

The traffic was light as many shops didn't open Saturday afternoons. Within minutes, they arrived at The Tusks, one of Mombasa's landmarks. Two sets of white elephant tusks towered over the four lanes of traffic. One set rose up to curve over the lanes in front of their car and the other set over the oncoming lanes. At the top, they crossed in giant arcs over the street.

Raheem hadn't spoken, so Ellen broke the silence. "Since I was a kid I've felt a child's magic each time I go under The Tusks."

"What kind of magic is that?"

"You'll laugh at me. I used to make up a story about giant elephants honoring me for driving though the great city of Mombasa."

"I'd love to hear your story. Right now I need something happy and funny in my life." Raheem made a sharp u-turn, and then drove into a narrow, dark alley that ended at the back of a building. He stopped in front of large, iron doors with "No Parking" painted across them in big, white letters. Ellen felt uneasy in the car alone with him.

"I've brought you here to show you what I own because it's all going to change. This building is part of the inheritance. Here at the back is a printing business I own." He pointed. "A cousin, my mom's sister's son, manages it. Let me open your car door."

As they walked back around to the front of the building, Raheem told Ellen about another business he owned, a large uniform shop where he employed tailors. "We make a lot of profit at that shop, especially when school starts."

In the alley stood several rancid-smelling garbage bins. Ellen stumbled over a pile of rubble and barely missed tripping over plastic bags that flapped in the black dirt. Two dirty white cats jumped out of a bin and crouched a few feet away, waiting to return to their dinner.

At the front of the building Raheem gestured his chin in the direction of the two shop doors. "One of the store fronts I rent out. The other is a bookshop my grandfather started years ago. I own it too."

Ellen interrupted him. "Hey, I buy books here all the time. I thought Muhammad owned this shop."

"He's the manager, another son of my mother's sister." He smiled at her. "I noticed a math book in the hands of one of the boys at your center. I recognized the sales tag on the back cover."

Inside, florescent lights brightly lit the store. A slight moldy smell filled the large room along with the scent of new books. On a table near the door, photography books of African animals sat in neat piles. On a revolving rack, colorful cookbooks were displayed. Best sellers and popular children's books filled shelves. Ellen knew this shop well, especially the basement where schoolbooks were arranged according to grade level.

Raheem said little. He led Ellen to the historical fiction section. "These were my father's favorite books—especially about India." He stopped. "And these," he touched the shelf below them, "are books I have spent hours studying."

"How Indians settled in East Africa?" she said.

"How we came in dhows—wooden sail boats—from India. I'm proud of what my family has done over the years." He turned to her. "I'm the last one to carry on our family legacy. But it's all ending, this business, our traditional home, our name…."

Ellen had never seen him look so miserable and sad.

"It's that curse. In a few months all this will be gone." He looked from one end of the shop to the other. Several workers had spotted him and were coming to greet him.

His lip quivered. He rubbed it. "I need to get out of here. Let's go down to Fort Jesus and sit on that wall. I need to explain what's going on. Wait for me at the door. I'll bring the car around."

5 Shattered Dreams

Saturday evening, October 7th

In less than a mile, Raheem and Ellen pulled into the parking lot at Fort Jesus. At the side of Fort Jesus a small patch of dirt provided a place where young men played football. A large group gathered around the dusty field and cheered their favorite players.

Raheem stopped for a moment to watch.

Old Town had few empty lots to play football. Mombasa, an island city, had been created by two inlets that pushed high tide waters into winding creeks and valleys. Years ago the inlets had met four miles from the sea. Now, a landfill carried a causeway wide enough for the Mombasa-Nairobi road. With land at a premium on the island, streets were narrow and crowded.

Cheers burst from the crowd. Players kicked up dust with their cleats and passed the ball back and forth for a goal. Raheem turned. "Even a good football game isn't cheering me." He seemed to be talking to himself. He pointed. "Let's walk down to the sea side of the fort. We can sit on a wall there and look out over the inlet where it meets the Indian Ocean."

"Raheem, do you know that under this dirt field is the rubble from excavations made in Fort Jesus? When the guys finish their game I'll show you little pieces of Chinese blue and white china from the sixteenth century."

"Really?"

"I've collected many of them."

"But what good are pot shards, only rubble, except to remind us of a life once lived in luxury?" Raheem sneezed from the dust. Ellen knew he didn't feel well. "Sorry, Ellen, It's just that I feel ruined. My dreams of being a doctor, serving people, owning a home have shattered."

"I'm sorry." She wondered what could be so wrong. They sat on the sea wall between two eight-foot cannons.

"What's happened?" Ellen finally asked.

"I don't want pity, but I need your prayers." He watched waves splash on the rocks below.

Ellen's heart ached to see Raheem so low. "How can I pray for you?"

Raheem's eyes swelled with tears. He kicked at a pebble under his shoe. "You are close to God and I need his help. My dreams, hopes, even my life crumbled last week. I'm...you see...I haven't been well. I was tested and told—Ellen, promise me you won't tell anyone, especially not my mother." Holding back tears, Raheem stared at the pebble.

Watching him struggle brought tears to Ellen's eyes as well.

"I won't tell anyone." She swallowed. "I hardly know your mother."

His voice trembled. "I have stomach cancer...it's spreading. For months I thought I had ulcers. Medical school, running several businesses, and the rentals, my mother—all of it is hard on me. I didn't get checked. I treated myself for ulcers. Now, according to tests, it's spread. I have...maybe two months to live."

A slight wind shook the leaves in a tree nearby. Ellen's heart trembled, hurting like an open wound. *This is why he's thin and pale. Why do I feel so deeply? I hardly know him.* "Raheem, I am so sorry."

He rubbed his eyes and swallowed hard.

Ellen tried to soothe him. "I'll pray every day for you. God will give you strength and peace through this terrible time."

Behind them the football players ended their game with loud cheers and headed home before dark.

Raheem fixed his eyes on the horizon. "You told me God can do anything. Remember on the plane, you said God can take away fear. I'm so afraid to die."

She touched his arm lightly. "I know he can take away cancer and fear."

They sat quietly for a moment. The sunset reflected a musty pink and the coming dark added to the feeling of gloom.

"God didn't create this world to be your home. He may be inviting you to his home."

"Paradise?"

"No, not paradise. I believe God made a special place for us in his own heaven. I hope I don't offend you, but isn't paradise where good Muslims live in a garden filled with virgins?"

He was silent.

"Having young girls around me for eternity would be quite tiresome."

"Ellen, I don't think you understand it. I'll ask Imam Ali to explain it to you."

"Maybe because I'm a woman I don't want to go there. I long to live forever with my loving and personal God. He stated in his Book that we'll rule and reign with him in a new and perfect universe."

"That sounds good to me right now."

They listened to the lapping waves below. Behind them the street lights flickered on. Slowly the whole city lit up like a swarm of fireflies.

"Dear God, Please help Raheem understand who you are. You can give him your peace." Ellen prayed silently, and then turned to him. "To get in God's home your name must be in his Book of Life. You must be his adopted child, that 'number one' child."

"I've considered my good deeds and my bad mistakes and I think the good outweigh the bad. But I can't know if Allah will accept me."

"Oh, God, I pray Raheem will believe you," she prayed silently.

Ellen grabbed his arm suddenly. "I love that word—accept."

"You have a way of going off the subject."

"No, hear me out. To accept is what it's all about. You do only one thing to be accepted by God. According to his Holy Book that one thing is to *accept* what God has done for you. He already forgave you. He took the punishment for your mistakes, your sins. Now he asks you only to accept what he did."

"I don't get it. Each person is accountable for his own sins."

"Yes. Every person deserves to be punished. But when God accepts us, his adopted children, it's not based on what we *do*, good or bad, Raheem. God accepts us when we accept what *he did for us*. He took our sins, and he was punished for them. He did this through Jesus. You've heard the story of Jesus dying a terrible death on a cross. Jesus is God, and in dying he was punished to pay for our sins so that when God sees us we are clean and forgiven. We just *accept* what he did and he makes us his adopted children."

"In Islam we are taught Jesus is not God, that God cannot die and that he could not pay for our sins."

"It's about God's perfect love. If I took your cancer into my body so you were free to live, wouldn't I love you? If I died for you, wouldn't I perfectly love you?"

He thought for a minute. "If it's as simple as that, I could believe it."

Raheem, she thought, *it is that simple!* She looked at him with a pleading look in her eyes. "It will change your life if you accept this. God gives his 'number one' children his spirit to live in them. His spirit helps you to know—really know God."

"You've made it clearer to me than before, but I need to think about it."

They stood up to walk back to the car. Raheem kicked at the dirt on the field.

"We'll have to look for pottery pieces another day. It's too dark." Ellen glanced into the night sky.

"I'm so afraid to die." Raheem hung his head. "When my mom finds out, she'll be impossible."

As they got in the car, Ellen turned to him. She hoped her words made sense to him. "When I get home tonight, I'll beg God to show you his power."

The streets of Old Town were lit by soft light. The enchanted sense of driving through four hundred years of history cheered them.

"I feel peace with you, even though we disagree about our beliefs. You have so much goodness."

I shouldn't be with this man. Ellen looked out the car window. *Yet, his suffering draws me to him.*

Then he added, "Thanks for coming with me. I need your calming spirit, especially now."

"What you see is God's calming spirit. I am not naturally calm."

"You're what God created you—beyond compare." For a second his eyes sparkled. "I've known you a short time, yet it seems I've known you all my life." He parked the car and opened Ellen's door. "Ali told me what you were like as a kid. I wish I had gone to Coast Academy." Raheem's gloom lifted. "And Naushad and his dad talked to me about your father. They remember him as a 'holy man.'"

Ellen hesitated at her gate. *I wonder what they said.*

"Last week I was thinking." He changed the subject. "I need to decide what to do with the businesses and rentals. Uncle Abdul is next in line to inherit them. I don't want him to have *any* of it. I hope I can donate books to your kids' center."

She was quiet. *He's thinking too much about me. How should I stop this?*

"Ellen, I don't want to make you uncomfortable. I want to be close friends, nothing serious. Is that okay?"

"I'll be your friend, but I must be honest. I—sort of—have a boyfriend."

Raheem kicked at the gate. "Another shattered dream."

They stood in silence. Then Ellen suggested, "You need a good friend from your community like Asmina—although she holds to the same beliefs I do."

"No, not her, I know her family. Her aunt wants her married. The way she stared at me, we could've had a proposal right there at Island Dishes." He tipped his head to the sky, light-reflected tears filled his eyes. "I'll never marry or plan a marriage, not with cancer." He dried his tears with his sleeve. "Ellen, please don't feel threatened by me or by a friendship with me. With cancer I must live one day at a time. There is no future for me. Just *be* my friend."

"That I promise. I will be your friend."

Monday, October 9th

On Monday at three in the afternoon Raheem and Naushad helped out at the kids' center. The kids screamed in laughter as the two blindfolded men stumbled around the room grabbing at the air, playing tag. At story time Raheem and Naushad acted out the main characters using silly expressions.

"We want Uncle Raheem and Uncle Naushad here every day," the kids begged Ellen.

Ellen hadn't laughed so hard in a long time. Her breath came in tight puffs. As she said good-bye to the children, she hugged each one.

After the kids left, Ellen invited Zillah, Mina and the two guys to the roof. Raheem admired the hanging garden. "Flowers, in full bloom, in the middle of Mombasa! I would have never believed it." He studied the plants and fingered one long leaf.

The setting sun splashed orange across the sky. The five friends settled in chairs and cooled down after the lively kids' program. City lights blinked on and a breeze swept away the heat.

"God paints the most amazing sunsets for us." Ellen leaned her head back against her chair.

"Sometimes I wish he would just talk to us instead of painting sunsets and flowers," Raheem waved his hands at the sky and plants. "I would love to have my many questions answered."

"In the *Injil*, or Gospels as we call them, God is called the Word. He came to talk to us."

After a moment, Zillah threw out a question. "Have you read the book called *John* in the *Injil*?"

"No." Naushad and Raheem said at the same time.

"Let me get a copy." Ellen left for a minute and returned with two books. "Tell me what you both think after you read it."

Mina's phone buzzed. Her Aunt needed her home to cook dinner. Zillah and Naushad also had to leave. Ellen had not intended to be alone with Raheem, and now she wished she had found a way to get him to leave with the others. It seemed he had something to say before he would leave. She turned on the patio light and stood by the stairwell gate.

"I have the birthday gift."

"I asked you not to give me a gift."

"You just gave me a book."

"And I gave one to Naushad too."

He drew a small blue jewelry box out of his pocket and flipped open the lid. In it laid a silver dove and chain. The light caught on sapphires embedded in the dove. Hues of blue caught the light perfectly. "This is what I think of you...you're like a dove."

"It's...beautiful!"

Ellen dared not look into Raheem's eyes. They would be hard to forget. Her impulses were unpredictable and she was fascinated by the changing shades of blue in the sapphires.

She laughed softly. "I flew into your life like a dove."

"Yes, but I am more impressed by your calm and peaceful spirit."

She knew she should not allow him to offer her jewelry. "I can't accept this. It's too expensive." Ellen protested. "I'm just a friend."

"I have two months...." He stopped and changed his sentence. "I can spend my inheritance any way I want. I chose blue sapphires so you'd remember me when I'm not around."

Ellen swallowed the lump in her throat that cut off her words.

"Please don't refuse my gift."

She lifted the necklace from the box and looked at it from all sides.

"Ellen." His voice grew deep and then he touched her cheek, tilting her face up to his. His fingers were soft yet strong. Her eyes met his—deep with longing, yearning to know his thoughts while a burning pulse ignited her heart.

This is so wrong.

He took the dove out of her hand. "Dove, it rhymes with…." He placed his hand on his heart for just a second then put the necklace back in its box and into her hands.

Ellen looked at the little box. "I'll treasure this gift, and more than that, I'll cherish our short friendship."

Raheem quietly said goodnight and left.

Later, alone in her apartment, Ellen once again fingered the necklace. What a meaningful gift! Raheem had a compassionate heart. For two months, they could be special friends. *But he's a Muslim.* Knowing the wild emotions and dreams would end soon was a sad relief. She blinked tears back. He wasn't for her. He was dying.

Raheem's health didn't improve in spite of Ellen's pleas to God. Five weeks passed. Raheem, too sick to leave his home, lay weak and frail as he stretched out on the sofa. Friends visited him daily. Ellen, Zillah, and Mina went as well. During visits they talked and joked about beliefs and customs, Americans and Kenyans. His knowledge of East African history fascinated Ellen.

One afternoon, he had the books *We Came in Dhows* on the coffee table. "These are favorites of mine," he said as Ellen skimmed their photos. "I want you to read them."

"Do you mind if I write your name in them? Books can be misplaced at the center. I'll return them in a few days."

Ellen thought about Raheem as she studied the books. She admired him, not for helping others, or being a doctor, and no longer for his good looks. He enjoyed friends and brought out their best even in his weakness. The kindness in his eyes never faded. He also felt responsible for his inheritance and spent long hours with his lawyer finding the right buyers for his rentals and businesses.

A few days later Ellen went to return Raheem's books. Mama greeted her and led her to the curtained door of Raheem's bedroom. She had never been in a man's bedroom, especially Raheem's. It was like entering his mind or soul and seeing all his secret thoughts.

"Ellen, come in."

"But it's your private bedroom."

"I have nothing to hide. You know me enough to forgive my faults and accept me the way I am." He sat propped up on pillows with an IV drip in his hand. "Sit on that swivel chair by my desk." She sat and slowly turned all the way around. The room was bigger than she had imagined.

A bookshelf, ceiling to floor, filled one wall stuffed with medical books, history books, and books on Islam. To the left stood filing cabinets and some wide shelves with a music system, computer printer, and copy machine. Financial charts were tacked to the wall. Above his bed hung a blown up photo of his family sitting by the ocean. On his bed sat a laptop. On the large, polished desk next to her, she saw the book, *John*, and an open notebook. He had outlined the chapters. Next to it laid the *Bible Knowledge Commentary*.

"Where did you get the commentary?"

"I found it on the Internet and ordered it. It clearly explains each verse within context and I like that."

"What do you think of the book I gave you?"

"I'm learning about God's unconditional love. I've never heard of this characteristic. If it's true, everyone would want his love."

"I pray every day that you'll accept it."

"Thanks. Two months ago I asked you to be my friend. When you visit and talk with me I feel peace even in my situation. Thanks for caring, Ellen."

Raheem's mother spoke as she looked around the curtain. "Abdul said he was coming today. He will be angry if he sees Ellen here. You are too weak to argue with him. Abdul said he's going to check on a cottage in Malindi tomorrow. Ellen, could you come back tomorrow?"

"Yes," agreed Raheem as Mama returned to the kitchen. "Uncle Abdul is doing all he can to take the inheritance. He doesn't know my plans for it. He's dangerous. You should stay away from him."

"I'll go then."

"No, wait. I'm working out a will. Two of the businesses have sold and the money is in a bank. My lawyer, Patel, is working out a trust fund. The problem is Uncle Abdul has a lawyer too. He'll bribe a judge who will change my will. I want most of the inheritance to go to charity—to your work."

"To my work? I don't mind getting some books, but money...."

A sad look came over Raheem.

"You don't want me dealing with your Uncle Abdul. When he finds that out, what will he do to me?"

"That worries me. I'm considering every possibility."

6   The Patient

November 20^(th)

Late Monday afternoon Ellen received a text message.

> *I'm in Mombasa Hospital.*
> *Pray for me.*
> *Raheem*

Before Ellen entered Raheem's hospital room, she prayed silently. *"Dear God, I'm nervous. Help Raheem heal."*

An attendant had just finished mopping the floor with disinfectant. Ellen rubbed her nose and then walked toward Raheem. His skin looked an awful chalky yellow as he lay on the white, starched sheets of the hospital bed. "Raheem, I'm so sorry. What can I do for you?"

"Sit and talk just like you always do."

She pulled up a chair until her knees touched the metal rails.

"Ellen, I'm a doctor but…I hate lying in a hospital bed." An IV tube draped from the back of his hand. "Do you mind if I complain? I've tried to live a good life for Allah. My father was even more devoted and we both got this cancer. If Allah looks at my good deeds, then why is he punishing me so severely?"

The corners of Raheem's chapped lips stuck together. Ellen reached for a plastic cup of water and held it to his mouth.

"I've lost hope. My faith has done me no good. It didn't help my father. What have we gained by our efforts? Look at Uncle Abdul—he's never once been punished for his million sins. What have I done to deserve this?"

Ellen could see his point. "I don't think God is punishing you. He's trying to get your attention. He wants you to see who he is. He created you to live with him forever, an eternal being."

"If I'm eternal, why is God cutting my life short?"

"A great man once wrote that each of us is like a thick, exciting novel, filled with drama on every page. The title page of that book is compared to the short time we live here on earth. The rest of the drama comes after we die. Imagine life in the presence of our loving God, enjoying him and working together in ways that human minds can't even grasp."

"Tell me again how I can get to this loving God of yours."

Raheem, please understand.

It would devastate Ellen if he died without knowing and accepting God's forgiveness. How many more chances would she have?

"Believe what God did for you. He took on himself the punishment for your mistakes, your sins, even your rejection of his love. Jesus is God who became a man but still was God. He died that terrible death on the cross. He died for you, giving his blood to pay for your sins. If you accept this gift, you are accepted by God and will live with him forever."

"I was taught we cannot know if Allah accepts us."

"That's a depressing position to be in."

"We don't believe Jesus was God and died and rose from the dead, either."

"Can't God do anything? His Holy Book says Jesus is God. Couldn't God come to earth and take our punishment? There is proof and you've seen it, Raheem. The proof is how God's spirit lives in those he loves. You've admired the peace and joy I have. That *is* God's spirit in me."

"I've admired that peace not just in you, Ellen, but in other people who believe the way you do."

Raheem's mother walked in clutching a big shopping bag to her chest. Tears filled her eyes. "Oh, my dear boy," she cried, leaning over him and brushing the hair off his forehead. "Are you all right? How do you feel?" She fussed over him.

"Tired. I don't like being the patient."

Ellen got up and offered the chair to Mama who eased her plump body into it. "Ellen, I'm glad you're here. Could you give me a lift, a ride home after my visit? My bag is so heavy."

"Sure."

"Ellen." A big man with a sweet smile stood at the door.

"Chaplain Kilonzo, how are you?" She shook hands with her father's friend. They had taught in the same high school.

"Raheem," Ellen turned to the bed. "This is Chaplain Kilonzo, a dear friend. He's great at encouraging people. Would you mind if he comes and prays with you?"

"We met this morning while I was being admitted."

Chaplain Kilonzo motioned for Ellen to follow him out to the hall.

"It's been a long time. How are your parents?"

"They miss Mombasa and especially teaching at the high school."

"Your Dad was a fine teacher." Kilonzo changed the subject and nodded toward Raheem's room. "How do you know this man?"

She described how they met and became friends.

"This morning we talked about his cancer and that he may not live through it. He is a doctor?"

"Yes." Ellen told Kilonzo about Raheem's inheritance and Uncle Abdul's curse.

It was turning dark outside. After saying good-bye to Raheem the group left together. Kilonzo helped carry Mama's bag out to the parking lot. Raheem called Ellen back as she reached the door.

"I had an idea. If you were my wife, Abdul couldn't take the money."

"Your wife?!"

"Not my wife, but if you signed a marriage license it would be very difficult for Abdul to get at my money."

"Raheem—no!"

"No?"

"No!"

"It'd only be a signature on a paper and the inheritance would be used wisely. Ellen, I'll be gone…soon."

"The answer is still no. Your mother is waiting. I have to go."

"Think about it," he called as she left.

The narrow streets of Old Town were built in the days of donkeys and camels and were never intended for motor vehicles. Even in Ellen's little VW bug, driving was tricky. She had to take wider streets and more round-about routes.

In her thick Indian accent, Mama whimpered next to her. "What will become of me? Raheem is my only child. His father died of the same, same cancer a year ago. We are cursed. You cannot know the pain in my heart. I cannot sleep. I take tablets for blood pressure."

Up ahead, the headlights lit up a wall. It looked like a dead end. Ellen stopped the car. Before this time she had walked to Raheem's house using alleys between the buildings and had not taken this road. Narrow streets closed them in on either side.

"Go left."

Ellen had to reverse to make the turn. Her side mirrors were inches from the walls.

"Why do those who do good suffer most?" Talking seemed to relieve Mama's grief. "My husband, he never lied, cheated, or drank. My sisters, they were jealous of me. He loved me, didn't look at other women even when I had only one child. In our culture that's not the custom. Yet cancer took him from me." She let out a bitter moan. "Now my son is dying."

"I know this is very difficult. But God knows all our sorrow because I believe he has gone through every hardship we experience. He is a God of great love. If you call to him, he will answer. He longs to help you."

"Will you pray to him for me?"

"I do, everyday, but he wants you to believe in him too."

Mama pointed ahead. "There, that is the back of our home. Park the car by that garbage bin."

Ellen carried the heavy shopping bag around to the wooden door. As Mama unlocked it with a big key, she sighed. She pulled on a string inside as they entered the wide hall. A yellow bulb lit up the entry.

She motioned Ellen to the kitchen. The room smelled of garlic and curry. Unloading her groceries, she continued to lament. "How can I live through this? Many times my husband's evil brother tried to persuade Raheem in his schemes and lies. But God kept him from mistakes. I tell you, he never cheated even on exams. You know, my son sat those long exams year after year."

Her distraught tone changed for just a second. "He made top marks," she smiled proudly. "It is Abdul who deserves to suffer. He should have cancer, not my good men."

Spent, she slumped into a chair and rocked her head. "Who will look after me? My sisters are married with families. Raheem, he promised to help me in old age. We used hard-earned money for him to become a doctor, to work in Mombasa. Now, no chance for his dream."

She looked at Ellen with pleading eyes. "Aren't there specialists—doctors who can help him? Doesn't one of them understand his kind of cancer?" Tears flowed down her worn cheeks.

"Mama, while I visited Dallas I met a cancer specialist. He attended my church and he is well known."

"Who is he?" She grabbed Ellen's arm. "I'll write him. I will do anything for my boy."

"I have my address book in the car. Let me get it."

Ellen pushed the wooden door open and ran around the building to the car. In her rush she nearly ran into a man leaning over her VW studying what was inside through a window. She backed up not sure if she should run or stand her ground.

Uncle Abdul turned. Anger lined his face. "I have one thing to say to you," he sneered. "If Raheem's will states that any of *our* family money goes to you, a judge will change the will. I have friends!" He clenched his fists at Ellen. "You stay away from here ore…!" He sliced his fingers in the air across his neck, turned, and walked into a dark alley.

Ellen's heart pounded as she quickly got the address book from the car and went back in the house.

"Here it is. Dr. Howard. He's about sixty-five years old, works at a big hospital called Baylor, and has helped cancer patients for over thirty years."

"I will try anything to help my son."

Ellen gave Mama the email and U.S. phone number. "Tell him I encouraged you to talk with him."

As Mama wrote the numbers, Ellen tried to comfort her. "God gave Raheem life as a baby. He allowed him to grow strong, to become a doctor, and to be a successful businessman. God wants you to trust him now. He has great mercy for those who believe him and love him. He longs for you to accept his love. He knows Uncle Abdul's heart and will give him what he deserves. God's justice is always right."

"Oh, how I pray Raheem's wealth will not go to his evil uncle. He is an alcoholic. He has his own corrupt money yet constantly begs us for more. He is jealous. He's probably spent all his stolen money on bribes."

"I can understand. I've met him—several times." Ellen glanced backwards over her shoulder and shuddered.

Each year at the end of November, over the American Thanksgiving holiday, Ellen attended a five day conference in Nairobi. This year she looked forward to it more than ever. The speakers were friends of hers from the U.S. and they had invited her to spend three days at Masaai Mara. Watching animals in the game parks was one of her passions.

She had also agreed to speak to the young singles at the conference. She had chosen to speak on living a pure life. About twenty singles attended each year and half of them Ellen knew from childhood.

She had booked the night train for November twenty-second and a return ticket ten days later.

Raheem still wasn't improving, even in the hospital.

A week and a half away from him is too long.

Ellen called several of her friends and asked them to take her place and speak to the young singles. No one could help her.

Ellen didn't want to go but she had no choice.

7 The Last Day

Wednesday, November 22ⁿᵈ

It was late in the afternoon and at seven that evening the train left for Nairobi. Ellen still didn't want to go. She decided to see Raheem at the hospital. First, she stopped by his doctor's office.

"I've done all I can," the doctor said. "He's not eating, and even with a tube he's not gaining strength." He looked at the floor and shook his head. "This is not what I hoped for."

"I'm going upcountry for ten days."

The doctor sighed, looking sadly at Ellen. "You might want to say good-bye before you go."

The thought of his death—gone forever—hit her hard. Her eyes swelled with tears as she bit her lip.

I could be back in six days and not go to Masaai Mara.

Ellen hurried to Raheem's room. She found him sleeping—the sheet wound tightly around his chest. He looked as though he'd already left this life. She sat in the chair by his bed. This could be her last visit with him.

She prayed silently. *"Oh, God, I wish I could do something. Please heal him. Lead him to yourself before it's too late."*

During her previous visits they had talked about Uncle Abdul. Raheem was repulsed by him. "I want to give the money to your work. Ellen, it's my dying wish, a gift to charity." He had told her Mr. Patel, his lawyer, had written a will; but they knew Uncle Abdul would change it.

Raheem had brain-stormed, thinking up anything. "Sign a marriage license. It's just a paper. It will be difficult to take the money from *you*." Her answer had been a strong no. He kept bring up the idea. "It's

51

only a signature on a paper," he had said. "I'll be gone in a week or two and you'll be free to marry whomever you wish. And if I give my money to charity, the Ashkar name would once again be honored."

Being married... even for two weeks, Ellen had refused.

"Nothing in your life will change. No one will know about the paper," Raheem had pleaded. "I do not want my money spent on drugs and alcohol, or bribing officials and paying thugs. He's a useless criminal."

Ellen forced these thoughts out of her mind and looked back to the bed. Raheem still slept.

Chaplain Kilonzo cleared his throat as he stood by the door. She greeted him in a whisper and motioned him quietly to the other side of Raheem's room. A door led to a balcony overlooking the Indian Ocean. Ellen and Kilonzo went out and sat on the balcony chairs.

Kilonzo spoke first. "The other day you asked me to pray with Raheem. I've come to like him. He's sincere, with a great love for people and a strong desire to know God's will. This morning we talked. He said his uncle is determined to change his will. He suggested that you sign a marriage license."

"He's asked me the same thing."

"I told him that you should only marry a man who loves God in the same way you love God. Raheem argued that it would be just a paper and not a marriage, a paper to save his inheritance from getting into the wrong hands."

"Can you imagine what my parents would think? How would I ever explain it? Married to a Muslim? We need to think of another way to help Raheem."

"Raheem asked me to sign the license, too. As a chaplain I can marry people. I told him it wouldn't be right."

From their place on the balcony, they noticed Mama come into the room. As she watched Raheem sleep, she began to cry. Ellen left Kilonzo's side to give her a hug. With her arm still around Mama, Ellen walked her out to join them on the balcony.

"He is very ill," Mama sniffed into a handkerchief.

"Yes, it's hard to see him this way."

Ellen tried to change the subject. She spoke softly. "Mama, what do you think of Raheem's wish to give his money to my work with the children?"

"Your work with the children is very good. Raheem is right to offer that money to help the poor." Mama took Ellen's hand and gripped it tightly. "You will not abuse the money; I know you."

"Wouldn't you like the money for yourself?"

"I have enough money to live a good life. If I took that money, Abdul...." Mama shook her head. "He would make my life miserable and without Raheem or my husband to defend me... no, no, no, I will not take that money."

Chaplain Kilonzo turned to Mama. "Raheem spoke with me about this. He said his uncle is determined to change the will. Raheem suggested that Ellen sign a marriage license."

"Yes, he told me this idea too. A marriage license will be harder to fight. It wouldn't be a true marriage—Ellen will not live with Raheem."

"I believe Ellen should marry a man who loves God in the same way she loves God."

"Would God disagree to this situation?" Mama looked into their faces. "It wouldn't be a real marriage, only a paper. This is Raheem's dying wish and he must die in peace."

Raheem stirred, letting out a low moan. Mama turned back into his room.

"Ellen, I have another appointment now." Kilonzo touched her shoulder. "Will you be here tomorrow?"

"No, I'll be in Nairobi for at least a week. I'm leaving tonight on the train."

"I think being away at this time will be good for you."

"But he's so weak. What if...?"

"God is in control."

Kilonzo and Ellen walked to the hall as Mr. Patel, Raheem's lawyer, arrived. They greeted him. Then Chaplain Kilonzo excused himself and left.

Back in the room, Raheem slowly moved his head from side to side as he woke up. "Why is everyone here? Is it my time—to go?"

Mama, sitting on the far side of the bed, kissed his forehead. "No, no, we just happen to be visiting you at the same time. How do you feel?"

"Weak. Ellen, come sit here." He motioned next to Mama. "Mr. Patel, how are you?"

"I have come with the papers you wanted, and the license. Musa and his brother are out in the hall."

Mama talked to Ellen in a whisper while Mr. Patel held up papers for Raheem to look over. "Musa is my sister's husband. He joined with his brother and they are buying the uniform shop and business. I am happy. Raheem is giving him a good deal and asking him to look after me. He is my favorite brother-in-law. Musa is also an Imam."

Patel called in Musa and his brother. They greeted Mama and Ellen then signed papers with Raheem. It took only a few minutes. They gently shook hands, lingering to hold Raheem's hand and praise him for his generosity.

"Wait for me in the hall," Patel said to the men as he gathered the papers into a file.

"I have one more paper." Patel looked around the room, then back at Raheem. "Now is a good time," he continued. "In court yesterday, I spoke to a friend, a judge, and I explained your situation. He sympathized with me and will help us." His voice lowered. "The license needs signatures."

"I am not sure she will agree," Raheem glanced at Ellen.

Ellen turned to talk with Mama and Mr. Patel said something to Raheem that she couldn't hear.

The next thing she knew Mr. Patel stood at the balcony door. "Ellen, may I speak to you?"

Mr. Patel and Ellen sat on the chairs. "Ellen, I had a serious talk with Raheem's doctor and he thinks the time is short, maybe less than a week. In a day or two Raheem may not be able to sign papers."

"This morning the doctor told me the same thing," Ellen replied. "Unfortunately, nearly a year ago, I planned to be at meetings in Nairobi this next week. I also planned a trip to Masaai Mara with a couple who are coming from the U.S. I feel I should cancel them."

They both grew quiet for a moment.

"As you know a signature on a marriage license makes it harder for Abdul to alter the will. If you are away at this difficult time, during Raheem's death, Abdul will assume you did not inherit Raheem's estate. Abdul will focus his efforts on Mama or others. This will give us time to process the will and transfer the money. All of us here today, Musa, Mama and I, know of Abdul's intentions and are determined to stop him. The two witnesses who sign the license would be Raheem's mother and myself. Musa is qualified to do marriages as well as the judge to whom I spoke. Musa could verify to the judge that the signatures are valid. The license would not be disputed."

Ellen folded her hands and looked at the floor. "I want to help Raheem and his family's reputation, but I don't want to do anything wrong. Can't we think of some other way to do this?"

"I'm not sure we can. Even if we could it would take time and we don't have time."

Mr. Patel took *The Daily Nation* paper from his bag. "I want to show you an article I read today. Look here on page five."

She read about four teenaged boys from a school near her kids' center who were taken by police. They had admitted to selling drugs in their school. Abdul Ashkar was suspected to be their supplier.

"When will he be stopped?"

"I wish I had his case." Patel said. "I could get international support, now that he's luring school kids into his schemes."

Mama rushed to the door gesturing up and down with her arms. "Come, come!" she whispered in panic. "Raheem is choking."

"Did you press the call button for the nurse?" Patel reached the bed at the same time Ellen did.

"Yes, but no one came."

"I'll get someone." Patel rushed from the room.

Mama grabbed some tissue from the bathroom and Ellen poured water into a glass.

"I'll be okay," Raheem stammered as he cleared his throat into the tissue.

The nurse arrived and helped him sit up. He coughed blood into the tissue. She helped him get comfortable and checked his charts. "Raheem needs rest now. May I ask that his visitors leave until he feels better?"

"Sister," Raheem cleared his throat. "Please let us have just ten more minutes."

"I don't think that's a good idea." She frowned.

"I'll be okay. I'm a doctor. I'll rest as soon as they leave."

"Fine, in ten minutes I'll be back." She left the room.

"Ellen, may I have a little of that water?" Raheem's face had turned an ashen white. "I'm sorry. I didn't mean to scare you."

Ellen looked at her watch. It was five-thirty. The train would leave at seven.

I'm leaving. I may never see him again.

"I'm going to Nairobi tonight for some meetings. I'll return as soon as I can."

"I know—you told me before. I'll try my hardest to be better when you return. If I'm not, I want you to have the…." Raheem looked at her, pleading. "It's just a paper and the money will be protected from Uncle Abdul."

How can I let evil Uncle Abdul steal the money? It's not a marriage. I'll never live with Raheem. Would it be so wrong to just sign a paper?"

Ellen glanced around at each person. Mama nodded in agreement. Mr. Patel moved closer to her. "We are all here, two witnesses, and Musa can verify the signatures."

Without thinking more about it, Ellen whispered, "I'll sign."

Mr. Patel wheeled the narrow bedside table to Raheem's side and asked Musa in from where he waited in the hall.

Raheem spoke softly to Ellen, "I may not last another week."

They signed the paper as the others looked on. Raheem's mother and the lawyer then signed as witnesses. Each one commented on how the paper protected the inheritance and that it was not a marriage between two people.

Again Raheem spoke to Ellen. "Thank you." He held his hand up. She gently shook it. "I'm at peace knowing your work benefits from the inheritance."

I wish I had peace.

Ellen trembled as Mr. Patel took her aside, "After Raheem has passed away, I will send for you. You'll be given a bank account."

What have I done? She didn't want to think about it.

Ellen rushed to her flat. She hardly had time to gather her luggage and get a taxi to the train by seven. The only thing in Kenya that left on time was the train.

In first class, she had a tiny compartment with a bunk bed and just enough room to stand. She noticed rips in the upholstery. The hot room smelled like bad breath. The fan didn't work. In fact it probably hadn't worked for the past ten years, she thought. She pushed on the water tap. No water came out.

An attendant knocked on the door and handed her what he called a 'torch,' a florescent flashlight. The first class car did not have electricity. With the flashlight propped on the seat she opened a copy of the license and read where Patel had filled in the blanks.

Groom: Mr. Raheem Ali Ashkar

Age: 27

Married to a man and I didn't know his age.

Religion: Muslim

Mother's name: Rahana Ashkar

That's a pretty name.

Legally, Ellen was now an Ashkar, related to the known drug baron! By law she had a new name. Oh, why had she signed without thinking about Abdul Ashkar? Dread filled her heart. What would he do to her if he found out? What would happen if *anyone* found out? She had to keep two secrets: her marriage, and the source of the money.

Another thought mulled in her mind. How could she speak on purity when she had a secret marriage?

Ellen felt her throat tighten. Was it asthma or just guilty panic? She couldn't talk to anyone about this...except Mama or Mr. Patel. Ellen dug for her phone in her purse and dialed Mr. Patel. "Please ring me the day Raheem passes away. And don't tell anyone about this license."

Being a widow would ease her guilt, but married to a...Muslim!

She buried her head in her hands and cried, "Oh, God forgive me. I feel so guilty!"

Saturday, November 25th

Three days later, at eight in the evening, Chaplain Kilonzo called. "Ellen, I am sorry, your good friend is gone. Raheem's mother took him out of the hospital this morning to die peacefully at home."

"Were you with him?"

"No. Early this morning I walked by his room. A doctor and several nurses were around his bed. It looked serious. They wouldn't let me in. Then I had to attend a relative's wedding, which took the rest of my day. I just got home and called the hospital to ask about Raheem. They said his mother took him home to die there. The nurse also said an Imam named Ali, Raheem's friend, had called to say he had passed away about five o'clock this evening."

"Will you attend the funeral?"

"The Muslim custom is to bury the body before sunset. I would have gone had I known. But I was at the wedding. I'm sure Raheem's mother and friends will be calling you tonight."

A second phone call came from Ali.

"I have sad news. It is the will of Allah." Ali paused. "I am sorry. Raheem passed away around five this evening."

"Were you with him?"

"Yes."

"Did he have any last words?"

"He went peacefully."

"How is Raheem's mother?"

"She is taking it hard. But we are arranging for all her needs during her time of mourning."

"Tell her I'm coming home Tuesday. I'll come see her then."

"Raheem's mother is with good friends; you don't have to rush back to help her."

The next day Mr. Patel called, "Ellen, my best client has left us. I feel a great loss. It is the will of Allah." He told her what Ali had said—that Raheem's mother took him home Saturday morning, and that he died peacefully that evening.

Ellen couldn't speak. She swallowed down tears as she listened to the lawyer.

"When you return to Mombasa, please stop by my office and I will arrange for your papers for the bank account. There are some other things to work out, including taxes."

As Ellen thought about the bank account and her last name, Ashkar, her mind went blank. Grief turned to regret. *"Oh, God, I'm a mess and confused."* She buried her face in her hands.

November 28th

Ellen returned to Mombasa Tuesday evening, exhausted and glad to be home. She walked over to see Raheem's mother but found the house locked and the windows shuttered. A neighbor said Mama Raheem had gone away and was not expected home for at least a year. "Mama couldn't live in that home alone."

On the way home she stopped at Island Dishes. Ellen stood at the counter and waited for Hatim as he served customers. On the counter, she saw a stack of books by the cash box. Ellen scanned the spines, *We Came in Dhows*. She pulled the books out and looked inside the front covers. In her handwriting, she found the name 'Raheem' written.

"Ellen, I'm so sorry." Hatim leaned on the counter. "He's better off now. He was so sick. It is the will of Allah."

"Did Raheem give you his books?"

"Ali gave them to me. He said Raheem's mother let him go through some of Raheem's things and give them to his friends. Do you want them?"

"No, you keep them." *I have a sapphire necklace,* she wanted to add. "Tell me what happened."

"I was off from work over the weekend. Some of my friends drove to a cottage up near Malindi. Naushad came with us. Ali had planned to come too but at the last minute he canceled. It's a good thing. It's our custom to bury before sunset and Raheem died late in the afternoon. Ali called us, but we were too late to get back to Mombasa before the funeral."

"Did you see Raheem's mother?"

"No. Ali helped her get a flight overseas to a friend's home. She couldn't stay in that house. She is also afraid of Abdul."

Ellen looked down to the floor and then back to Hatim. "I need to get home. It's getting late. Will you walk me?"

Life had changed so fast. Raheem was gone; his mother had disappeared now, too. Sadness swelled in her heart because she feared neither had accepted Jesus' love.

8   Norman

Friday, March 23rd

In March, the hot season in Mombasa wheezed its humid, sticky breath on every soul. It crept into each alley, building, and room. The salty dampness chipped paint from walls, rusted iron, and corroded plastic. The weather's biggest offense—mold—spoiled clothes, food, and books. Cupboards were kept open, and twenty-watt bulbs were installed to keep the odious mildew out.

The heat and humidity stifled the breath out of the strongest person. Shopkeepers and businessmen took long naps at lunch hour. Dinner was served between eight and nine o'clock and bedtime always came late.

Ellen checked her email and found that Norman Gilberts had written.
> Dear Ellen,
> You left in September.
> Six months seems forever.
> I clearly remember
> The day we were severed
>
> Wow, I'm writing poetry to you.
> I can't wait for the day I see you again.
> Hey, hey, that day is in one week. Am I hyper or what?
> You asked me to write about my expectations.
> I want to help with the kids and your work.
> I want to lead ....

Norman, the youth pastor at her church in Dallas, had arranged a team of two men and three ladies to fly out and help Ellen. Ellen especially looked forward to Mrs. Howard, the sixty-five-year-old doctor's wife.

She read on.

> A huge expectation is time with you.
> I miss you and want to build our relationship.
> Please plan time for just us. I believe
> God wants our friendship to grow deeper.

Ellen stopped reading and tried to feel the tender affection she once felt for him.

Do I want a deeper friendship with Norm? We did date in college. Where's that spark I once knew?

Since Raheem's death Ellen had found it hard to focus. She avoided people like Chaplin Kilonzo. Even Mina and Zillah noticed her lack of energy. She worried about her listlessness, while memories of Raheem filled her mind. Five months had passed and she had improved, some.

But the excitement and spark she had felt for Raheem wasn't there for Norman. *Will this visit with Norman lead to the end of their friendship? Will I feel awkward around him? A break up?*

She remembered that feeling—the hurt and pain of breaking up. Rick Davidson. How many times had she broken up with him? Ellen liked Rick. Their families had been friends since she was little. He was fun, and a tough guy. At times—wild! Girls liked him and he dated them. Ellen had nicknamed him 'Roaming Rick' and he called her his 'forever friend.' He loved romantic settings, and the word 'serious' was not in his vocabulary.

She looked again at Norm's email. Norm. He did everything just right and followed his plan to the second. The unexpected stressed him.

Ellen wrote down the flight number and time of his arrival. She'd arrange for a van to pick up the team at the airport.

Friday, March 30ᵗʰ

A week later at the airport, Ellen spotted Norman at the 'arrival' door. He dropped his bag and dashed over, his cowboy boots clomping on the cement floor. With arms flung apart and mouth wide open, he grabbed Ellen around the waist and twirled her in the air. Norman appeared overjoyed to see Ellen.

With a huge smile, he introduced each teammate. "This is Tim, a medical student." Tim took Ellen's hand with both of his.

Another doctor, thought Ellen. *He has kind eyes.*

Norman continued, "Darla is our church secretary and works with me."

Ellen said, "I remember you from church in Dallas."

Darla nodded silently. Her long, brown hair was tied in a tight ponytail.

Norman turned to the last person, "Melissa just moved to Dallas. She is a trainer at a gym." She stood tall and gave Ellen a wide, friendly smile.

"Where is Mrs. Howard?" asked Ellen.

Melissa answered. "She stayed in Nairobi to visit a hospital Dr. Howard sponsors."

Norman dug in his pocket and pulled out a scrap of pink paper. "Mrs. Howard sent a note. She's stopping by Mombasa for a few days before she flies down to Dar es Salaam. She has more friends to visit down there."

Ellen groaned. "I looked forward to having Mrs. Howard's experience." She needed an older, mature person on the team. It would stabilize the group.

With four carts of heavy luggage, they pushed toward a crowd of waiting people on the sidewalk. Six taxi drivers approached them, talking all at once.

"Taxi?"

"Good price, my friend."

Ellen led the group through them, graciously declining all offers. "I hired a *matatu,*" she explained.

Tim pointed to the parking lot. "Why are the cars so far away from the airport building?"

"Vehicles aren't allowed near the building, even to pick up people," Ellen said. "This precaution started in 2004 when terrorists attempted to shoot down a plane here with a hand-held missile."

"Wasn't a hotel bombed, too?" Tim caught up with her.

"It was the Paradise Hotel, owned by Israelis, north of here. We won't be going up that way."

"How many people were killed?"

"I think about thirteen. Let's talk about something else." Ellen wanted everyone to feel safe.

She noticed Darla clenching her purse and her face looked drawn with worry. "Darla, how are you doing?"

"It's my first time for everything and I'm petrified. That was even my first time flying." She tucked her blue plaid shirt into her long jeans skirt. "I want to see everything, but I'm scared to death."

Melissa strolled ahead talking to several baggage handlers who had grabbed her cart. She laughed as they mimicked her accent.

Darla stopped and waited for Norman. The wheels of his heavy cart caught on the uneven sidewalk.

Tim came up beside Ellen. "What vehicle are we taking?"

"See that van with the yellow stripe?" She pointed. "It's called a *matatu*. I hired it with a driver and tout to drive us to the guesthouse."

"A tout?"

"He collects the fares. The driver only drives the van. That's the Kenya law. It gives people more job opportunities."

After the tout piled the luggage up to the ceiling in the back seats, he asked Norman to sit up front. Norm looked at Ellen with I-want-to-sit-by-you eyes. She whispered in his ear, "In Kenya the eldest person is given the place of honor. He's trying to respect you."

Norman huffed and climbed in front.

At the parking ticket booth, they waited in a long line.

Tim kept asking his non-stop questions. "Look, several cars are going out of the airport using the lane to come in. Why is that?"

"It's just faster. People in the booth take tickets from that lane too if there are no on-coming cars."

Norman couldn't believe it. "So you mean cars just push ahead in the wrong lane?"

"Unfortunately the aggressive person is accommodated and taking turns is not always important."

As they headed for town, Norm spoke loudly from the front, "Whoa, whoa, get a look at that pot hole! It's all the way across the road."

Tim, sitting next to Ellen, pointed out the window. "Those large trucks must dig up the asphalt." In a customs depot lot to the right, forty-foot-long steel containers, blue, red and gray, were stacked four high. Large trucks waited in line to load the containers onto their beds.

Ellen smiled. "I'm not used to American words. Kenyan English is so different. Kenyans call big trucks 'lorries' and asphalt is called 'tarmac'. Thousands of truckers transport goods from Mombasa port to at least six other countries."

Tim laughed. "Lori, that's my sister's name."

Another *matatu* cut in front of their van and then suddenly stopped to collect a person waiting by the curb. Their driver slammed on his brakes and the team lurched forward.

Again in a loud voice, Norman turned and said, "Hey, that van in front of us didn't have brake lights! Is that another not-so-important thing in Kenya?"

Darla, curled up with her face wrapped in her sweater, cried out, "I can't look. This is stressing me out. How long 'til we get there?"

"Twenty minutes to the ferry, then we wait to get on it. The ferry ride is only a few minutes. Amani Acre guesthouse is two miles from there." Ellen patted Darla's arm. "You'll make it. It's not that bad. We're going to be at the beach! You'll have your own room."

"Alone! Oh, please don't put me alone," she begged.

Melissa hung out the sliding window. "This is Africa. We are in Africa!" She waved to a man pushing a cart filled with tomatoes.

Lorries parked in a line along the shoulder of the road. The dirt under them oozed with black oil.

Norman shook his head. "I can't believe it. They drain the old oil onto the ground."

"Look, the local Michelin™ dealers." Melissa laughed, pointing to a small stick hut with yellow plastic tied over it. Three men sat slouched in big truck tires. More tires were stacked behind them.

Norman added, "And look at all the trash, especially the plastic bags."

A strong reeking stench of burnt plastic and rotting garbage filled the air. "I think I'm going to throw-up," Darla complained. Even Melissa held her nose.

Ellen, a little frustrated with the group, tried to explain. "We are crossing a man-made causeway made of garbage land-fill. I will never understand why the government welcomes us to Mombasa with this disgusting odor."

Mombasa's buildings were mostly two stories, shops on the ground floor with apartments over them. Outer walls were grayish black; mold hid their paint. Others had wall-to-wall bright advertisements splashed across them. *Crown Paints* colored buildings in bright rainbows. *Safaricom* painted buildings in green and competed with the red colors of *Celtel* as they both advertised mobile phone access and packages. *Trust* advertised condoms with lovers face-to-face on a background of deep blue and orange.

"What's *Trust*?" Norman asked.

Ellen leaned forward and whispered, "With Kenya's HIV problem, condoms are widely advertised." Norman's neck turned a pinkish red.

In the town center, eight *matatus* to every one car hooted, pushed, and blocked traffic as they tried to make the two-lane street into three lanes. Touts shouted to people standing on the curbs, "*Feddy feddy,*" and "*Doxs, doxs,*" hissing out the x.

"What are they yelling?" asked Tim.

"*Feddy* means the route to the ferry and *doxs* to the port."

The air smelled like the salty ocean as they arrived at the line for the ferry. Venders reached into the window trying to sell beaded jewelry, soapstone carvings, and cashew nuts. On the sidewalk, more vendors held up men's handkerchiefs, razor blades, and bright lengths of cloth used for ladies wrap-a-rounds.

Melissa jumped out to take photos. "Can we dress in those wrap-a-rounds while we're here? They're so cool."

Ellen encouraged Darla to get out too. She leaned on the van door by Norman while quietly watching the loading of a ferry. Forty vehicles squeezed into narrow rows on the ferry's flat floor. Then three thousand passengers on foot moved like a wave of humanity on to the prow and into spaces between the cars.

Darla covered her mouth in alarm. "No, no, we aren't getting on that. It could sink!"

"This can't be real." Norman bit his thumb nail. "People are so packed, standing shoulder to shoulder. Doesn't anyone go mad with claustrophobia?"

"Look, Darla," Ellen pointed, "another ferry's coming. People cross here everyday. I wouldn't take you across if I thought we'd sink."

"I've never been on a ferry. I'll get seasick." Darla grabbed Norman's arm.

"We need to pray," Norm whispered.

Ellen looked at Norman. His eyes were wide.

"Dear God…" he began.

Ellen didn't listen.

I need to ignore a lot of their fears. They feed off each other's imaginations. They will be fine in the end.

It was dark when they drove into the compound of Amani Acre, a guesthouse on the Indian Ocean. *Amani* meant peace in Swahili. The guys shared an apartment divided by a wall from the girl's larger cottage. Darla's room had an extra bed and Ellen decided to spend the night. She'd help lessen their anxieties and orientate them to Mombasa life.

Melissa ran out to the gate facing the Indian Ocean and then back. "Guys, you got to see this! It's a huge orange glow, like a UFO on the horizon."

An arc of white moon thickened steadily over the water. Within seconds a glowing bright ball faced them. The sea reflected a silver moonbeam, a long, shimmering line that extended all the way to the shore. Coconut trees rustled their branches overhead and a sea bird pitched a cry up the beach. They stood in awe in the warm sea air.

Norman stood by Ellen. "You didn't tell me about this."

"No. It's too romantic." She smiled up at him. "You came to *work*," she teased.

"True." He smiled back. "I *am* here to work." His eyes gazed at her under his thick blond eyebrows. "I work during the day, not evenings. God's beautiful moonlight is here for us. I think it's a sign." He touched her arm. "Let's sit at the picnic table and talk."

He looked good—tall and strong in the moonlight. "Along with work, let's plan time together."

"I'll work side-by-side with you all twelve days." Ellen still teased.

He reached out and touched her hand. "It's been six months since I've been with you."

She let him tuck her smaller hand in his larger one.

Where is that spark? Ellen sighed. *I've changed.*

"Norm, one constant in Kenya is that plans change." She looked in his eyes. "We'll need to be flexible."

"You know that's hard for me. Now, tell me, what do you have scheduled for us?—and I realize even that could change."

Ellen had planned kids' activities to start at noon each day and end around six. The team would be free every morning. For the weekend she'd planned they prepare and take charge of the Easter program.

"Every morning off? That's a lot of free time."

"You asked for time." She smiled.

The moon had climbed higher. "Just look at that!" Norman whistled. "I've never seen it this bright. The coconut trees have shadows."

Melissa and Tim stood talking near the gate to the beach. Darla had gone back in the cottage.

"Nothing compares to this. It's enchanting."

"Be careful, Norm, you could fall in love with a coconut tree."

"I'm falling in love, but not with a tree." He turned to face her, a soft smile on his lips.

A scream erupted from the cottage. "It's Darla!" Ellen jumped up from the picnic table and ran across the yard to the cottage. Norman followed close behind her.

Darla, shivering and cowering, stood on a chair in the kitchen while pointing to a trail of black and yellow ants, each about an inch long.

"I turned on the light." she cried, "and they came out from that little cupboard."

Norman opened the kitchen door to the backyard, picked up the small cupboard, and manhandled it through the door and out onto the grass. On the floor where the cupboard had stood swarmed a nest of a hundred ants with their rice-size yellow eggs.

Darla screamed louder.

"Darla, calm down. They won't hurt you." Ellen grabbed a can of *Doom* insecticide from the top of the refrigerator. The ants scattered farther over the kitchen floor as she sprayed them. Then she swept them into a dust pan, giving the wiggling insects one last dose of insecticide before she tossed them out the door into a hedge.

Darla remained on the chair while Norman, Tim and Melissa watched.

Ellen tried to explain. "Some people call them sugar ants and some say wood ants because they build their nests in wood. They're harmless. They come out at night when the lights are off and look for sweet bits of food. I think every house in Mombasa has them."

"Will they get in my bed?" Darla whined.

"They only like kitchens."

The manager, Aunt Martha, and a guard appeared at the door. "Are you all right?"

"We're fine. Just getting used to African insects." Ellen shrugged.

"What's the cupboard of glasses doing out in the yard?" Aunt Martha nodded to the discarded cabinet.

Norman hurried out. "I'll return it." As he picked it up they heard the sound of broken glass. "I'll pay for the glasses as well," he added sheepishly.

9   Abdul Ashkar

Wednesday, April 4th

Five days later, feeling exhausted, Ellen stretched out on her sofa. Asthma had kept her awake in the night. The air smelled of thick humidity. In the early morning hours the first rain after the long dry season had fallen with big droplets beating the dust and soaking into every nook and cranny. Raindrops had oozed into cracks, chasing out the mold spores that triggered Ellen's asthma.

It was lunchtime and Norman's team, who had gone sightseeing for the morning, was meeting at her flat. The rain had stopped hours ago, but a leak still dripped by her coffee table. Ellen had placed a bucket under it. Now she searched through the yellow pages and dialed a roofer.

"Who are you calling?" Norman's booming question made her jump. He walked into the room.

"The roofers." Ellen pointed to the bucket and then the ceiling.

"Isn't that the landlord's responsibility?"

She spoke into the phone. "Yes...this afternoon...an estimate. I need the roof repaired this week. Yes, I have the cash."

Norman had that all-too-familiar I-don't-believe-this look on his face. "Why on earth are you calling a roofer, arranging an estimate, and paying for the job?"

"If I don't get it fixed now, it'll be worse when it really starts raining."

"No, no, this is not your responsibility. You need a man around here...anyway, the landlord should pay for this."

Ellen looked at him with a blank stare. She compared the frown on his face with the kind, giving eyes she missed so deeply. She couldn't think of something nice to say.

71

"Where are you getting that much cash?" Norman demanded.

"I was given plenty of repair money."

"From whom?"

"From my landlord's good friend."

"Your landlord's good friend? A Muslim?"

How would he ever understand Raheem's kindness and generosity? A fresh pain spread through her heart. She looked at the water collected in the bucket. Such a tiny bit of water created such a huge problem.

"Norm, I really do have the money. I know you don't like it when I am impulsive, but this is—"

"The roof should be the landlord's expense. If you have money, let me suggest you spend it on a new car."

Ellen frowned. "What gives you the right to insult my car?"

"It's old, rusty, and noisy...you deserve a decent car."

"My father gave me the Volkswagen when he retired. It has memories...it's precious, a family heirloom."

Darla, Tim and Melissa came through the door. Darla vanished into the bathroom.

Melissa stretched her arms out behind her back. She plunked down beside Norman on the sofa. "Norm, you should have come. The camel ride was awesome."

As Melissa told him about their morning, Norman removed his tight cowboy boots. He splashed water from the bucket on his swollen, sweaty feet.

Ellen thought about Norman as she watched his actions. She considered that he fit what she wanted in a man. He loved God and had given his life to serve God, not his own ambitions. He was a great leader, loyal, trustworthy, and kind.

But he's hyper and detailed. I need flexibility.

Norman interrupted her thoughts as he spoke to the group. "I had an interesting morning in front of Fort Jesus. I met this guy...actually he came up to me and started asking questions."

Is he preaching at Fort Jesus like a street evangelist? Is he disturbing the peace?

Why am I thinking so badly about him?

Tim whispered to Ellen. "I think there's a problem." He motioned to the bathroom.

"Sick?"

"No, maybe, ah…emotional?"

Ellen knocked on the bathroom door and asked Darla to let her in. Norm called after her. "The guy at Fort Jesus said he knows you, Ellen. He kept asking where you get money to help the kids."

At the same moment, Zillah and Asmina arrived with the food for lunch.

"I'll get to you all in a minute. Let me help Darla first."

Darla sat cross-legged on the bathroom rug with her arms on the tub, sobbing.

"I just can't…I can't handle this. It's too freaky. Look." A line of red spots crossed her stomach. "I'm losing it." She let out a pathetic moan and ferociously scratched her neck. "Last time I got this tense a blood vessel in my eye burst and I was taken to the emergency room."

Ellen sat on the floor with Darla. "Take a deep breath. There, breathe in—now out. Try to relax." Darla scratched her neck, but did as ordered. Ellen flipped Darla's long hair up over her head and found more red dots.

"You'll feel better when we get something on those itchy bumps."

"I'm allergic to most medications."

"Darla, trust me. I can help you."

Ellen opened the bathroom door and motioned to Zillah. She handed her some money and sent her off to a nearby shop. Zillah returned in minutes with a white plastic bottle. In the kitchen, Ellen poured pink liquid from the bottle into a dainty china teacup. She placed the matching saucer under it.

Norman, still talking about the man he met at Fort Jesus, called to Ellen. "He kept asking about you. You must know him. He has a serious scar on his neck. He's invited me back tomorrow."

Ellen nearly dropped the cup.

Uncle Abdul Ashkar! Norm, talking to that evil, treacherous man, telling him everything about me!

A flood of anger swelled in Ellen.

"I'll be right back."

With the china cup clattering, she opened the bathroom door and slammed it shut. Darla, still leaning against the tub, moaned.

Ellen had lost her patience. "It's hard for me to believe you are crying this hard because of a rash. Tell me—honestly—what's wrong."

"I'm so miserable I hate myself." She whimpered blowing her nose. "I'm emotionally mixed up…in love with someone I shouldn't be thinking about. I've been living a lie. This whole week…"

Ellen waited for her to go on, but Darla had said enough.

"So, you're in love with the wrong guy."

Darla nodded and sobbed.

Ellen smiled a little smile. "Then I know exactly how you feel. I did the same thing with a handsome, rich, Muslim doctor." A faraway look came over her face. "It ruined my life." She shook her head. "It ruined everything: my dreams, my mind, emotions, even my name."

Darla stopped her fussing. "You? Are you still seeing him?"

"No."

"See," Darla sobbed. "That's my biggest problem. I can't let go. Everything about this guy is perfect."

"If he's so perfect, why aren't you with him?"

"I am with him!"

She's in love with Tim.

"You'll hate me. I—it's Norman."

Darla and Norman. Why not? Why didn't I see it before?

Darla's words tumbled out. "I'm with him at work and I can't help it. I…I know he likes you. He talks about you to everyone. When you get married, I'll never have a chance to…so I came with the team. I came because…I'm such an idiot!" Darla started to cry so hard Ellen feared a blood vessel would break. She placed the china cup and saucer on the floor and turned Darla to face her.

"Darla, listen. Promise to keep a secret?"

She nodded.

"I will never marry Norman. So, with God's help, you can have him." Ellen surprised Darla and even herself with her declaration. *Do I know what I am saying? I haven't thought this through.*

Ellen knew Norman was a good man. But what were her true feelings for him? She didn't feel…that excitement she had felt around Raheem.

Will I regret this?

"But he loves you," Darla said.

"He does. But you and I are going to change his mind." She gave Darla a gentle hug.

"Now, those itches need what's in this china cup. It's a special bath lotion wealthy people use to get rid of bites. Get up. Take a nice shower and scrub with this lotion. We are eating lunch in fifteen minutes."

Ellen left the bathroom and sat down across from Norman.

I have a painful breaking-up speech I need to give you, she thought. Frustration and anger still nettled at her.

Melissa, still sitting on the couch, read *The Daily Nation* newspaper. "U.S. Marines are guarding freighters, cruise ships, and even local dhows in the Indian Ocean from attacking Somali pirates. How cool! I want to be a Marine."

"Speaking of dangerous…." Ellen looked at Norman. "I think you are putting me in danger."

He frowned. "How's that?"

"The man you met at Fort Jesus, Abdul Ashkar, is a drug baron. Five months ago his nephew died. The nephew, kind and compassionate, knew about the children's center and willed his inheritance to it. He did it so Abdul wouldn't waste the money on illegal businesses. Abdul doesn't know his nephew gave money to this work. He's a dangerous man. Don't talk to him again. Don't even go to Fort Jesus."

"How much money did you inherit?"

"A lot! He had several well-run businesses."

"Was your landlord's friend that nephew?"

"Yes."

"The man at Fort Jesus mentioned knowing your lawyer."

"Knowing my lawyer?" Ellen raised her hands to her chest in panic. *Is Abdul talking with Mr. Patel? Does he know about the marriage license? But Patel was Raheem's lawyer. I don't have a lawyer.*

"Did he mention my lawyer's name?"

"I don't remember."

"What did he say about my lawyer?"

"Nothing, he just said he knew him. The man seemed to know you so well—in a good way." Norman's face changed to worry as the information sank in. "Ellen, I'm sorry—"

She cut him off. "I don't want to talk right now."

Ellen stood, leaving Norman where he sat on the sofa. She went out to the patio where Zillah and Mina prepared a table for lunch.

Tim came and stood by her. "What medication did you buy for Darla?"

"A special bath lotion called *Wadudu Kill*. It gets rid of itches." Ellen bit her lower lip. "It's dog shampoo. I told her wealthy people use it. I just didn't explain it's for their dogs."

He smiled at her with approval. "Just what the doctor ordered."

"It works for everything, including camel fleas." Ellen wanted to laugh, but she was still upset. They walked together to the corner wall where Tim leaned in close.

"Ellen, are you all right? It's not easy coping with your work, the people, and all the problems. Just living here is hard."

"At the moment, I'm struggling," She admitted with a sigh. *Is it so obvious? Will I ever have peace again?*

"Are you and Norman having a—"

"Tim." She turned to face him. "You know him. Do you think—are Norm and I right for each other?"

"Norman is a great guy. I respect him. You're an incredible woman. I've never met someone as passionate for God as you are. I think God has each of you exactly in the right place. But I don't think those places are on the same continent."

Ellen's phone buzzed, interrupting them. She excused herself and flipped it open.

A deep voice growled, "Helloooh. Is this Ellen?"

"Rick! I know it's you. I'd know your voice anywhere!"

10 Rick

Wednesday, April 4th

"Do you have time for a visitor?" Rick asked Ellen over the phone.

"Where are you?"

"I'm in Nairobi. How is the train these days? I got a ticket for Mombasa. It leaves tonight."

"The food will give you diarrhea and the seats are torn."

"Oh, come on. Isn't it romantic, like the 1920s train from the *Out Of Africa* movie?"

"Sometimes it doesn't even arrive and you have to get a bus from where it stops."

"Now you tell me."

"Rick, I didn't know you were in Kenya."

Rick Davidson, the same age as Ellen, had grown up in Mombasa and had attended school with her. When he went off to college, his parents moved to Uganda. While visiting them on the border of Congo, Rick had become interested in gold mining. He had joined a company and done well. He thrived on the action and adventure his job demanded in Congo's remote jungle.

"I'm planning a dhow trip to Dar es Salaam, one of my big dreams. How are the dhow trips these days?"

"I have no idea. I never thought of sailing on one."

"I'll be in Mombasa for a week. It'll take me time to work out the trip. I need to find a captain willing to have me aboard. Ask around for me, will you?"

"Where will you be staying?"

"I'm booked at the New Palm Tree Hotel." His voice changed. "Ellen, I'm coming to spend time with you, too. Our first date will be the

Fort Jesus Sound and Light Show. Don't say no, because I've called and made reservations for tomorrow evening."

"Rick you haven't changed a bit."

"Meet me at the train station tomorrow morning? I have my *piki-piki*. Remember that old BSA six-fifty motorbike? But I can't carry my luggage on it."

"And I have my dad's old VW bug, remember it?"

"What a sweet little car. I'm mostly coming to see you. Don't answer now, but consider sailing on the dhow with me."

At eight-thirty the next morning, Ellen parked her white, rusty car on the gravel lot at the train station entrance. The small building, built in the 1920s, had a red tile roof and wood-paneled walls. Its wide entrance led straight through the building to a double door opening out to the track. She could see the train. Most of the passengers had gotten off. The baggage car stood next to the engine.

Rick, sporting a slight beard and huge hairy arms, pushed his big black bike down the wooden planks off the baggage car. He had thrown his jacket over his shoulder. Next to him, a Kenyan man in a khaki uniform pushed a squeaking, two-wheeled, wooden cart with Rick's two black duffle bags threatening to slide off. Taxi drivers crowed at the entrance. "Taxi! Taxi! Where to?" The squeaky cart separated a path through the crowd.

In the parking lot, Rick kicked the stand and parked the black bike next to the white bug. Ellen extended her hand for the traditional Kenyan greeting. "How are you, Rick?"

"How about a big hug from your old boyfriend?" He gave her a one-arm squeeze around the shoulders. "You are ageless, and that brings good memories."

"Thank you."

"I've been thinking a lot about this moment, seeing you, being back in Mombasa. I've missed you."

He looked older; little wrinkles fanned out from the sides of his eyes. It made him look happy. His six-foot body, tan and rugged, looked even stronger than she remembered.

Rick, my best friend and worst enemy, how do I feel about you? It's always a mix.

At the New Palm Tree Hotel they ordered mid-morning tea on the roof's patio. They sat on white deck chairs with little tables next to them. A breeze filtered through the green potted plants and across the red floor tiling.

They discussed the dhow trip to Dar es Salaam: finding a captain, and what food, bedding, and supplies to take.

"It's not fun going alone. Ellen, take a few weeks off and come with me."

"I have a team from the States here for another week. We have programs planned."

"It'll take me a week to prepare to sail. This will work out perfectly. Your team leaves for the USA and then we sail on a wooden dhow to Dar es Salaam. How about we go via Zanzibar?"

"That would be an adventure."

"I hope you've got time for me, too—this week."

"You've come at a busy time."

At ten-thirty Ellen returned to the team. Norman met her on the stairway to her flat. "You said the train arrived at eight-thirty." He looked at his watch. "What took so long?"

"We had tea. We haven't seen each other in years. And, Norm, I plan to go out tonight as well. I know I'm taking time I promised you, but you've all come to Mombasa on the same week. Please understand, Norm, please?"

Norman sulked with his hands in his pockets. "We have only seven days left."

That evening Rick and Ellen met at the New Palm Tree Hotel where a taxi collected them. Ellen dressed in a light blue and silver Punjabi outfit. The sapphire dove hung around her neck.

The taxi driver zigzagged around potholes and through a coconut grove. A few miles up the inlet they came to a large old British bungalow. Out from the veranda spread a lawn, then a long stairway down to the inlet. A wooden dhow was tied to the pier.

"I never imagined The Sound and Light Show starting here. It's beautiful," Rick commented.

On the pier, three men in bright red and orange shirts performed sixties hits on guitars and skin-covered African drums.

Rick took Ellen's hand and stepped up through a little door onto the dhow's deck. Everything was made of wood, even the pulleys holding the ropes to the sail.

Soft red velvet cushions covered the benches built along the side of the boat. Rick led Ellen to the front and then sat close to her. "Ellen, you've got to sail with me to Dar es Salaam."

A waiter served fruit drinks from glasses trimmed in sugar crystals. A plate of finger foods offered roasted peanuts, vegetable *samosas*, small carrot sticks and a thick slice of cucumber hollowed out to hold cucumber dip.

"Mmm, there's a kick to the *samosas*—hot chili." Rick said with his mouth full.

Ellen rubbed the red peanut skins off and tossed them over the side of the boat. As they floated atop the water, a fish nibbled at them.

Raheem wanted to take me here. She sighed.

The sunset brightened the light blue sky as an orange glow fell on the mangrove trees lining the inlet. Colors mixed and changed in perfect harmony as they reflected in the water.

"This is part of the Light Show painted and performed by God," Ellen said watching the sky.

After an hour of blissful sailing along the inlet the dhow docked at Old Port on the edge of Old Town. City lights turned on like stars. A huge spotlight lit up the gangplank.

"This pier is where hundreds of Indians, Arabs, Western explorers, and missionaries took their first steps into Africa," Ellen said as they stepped off the dhow on to the pier.

Rick took Ellen's arm. "Let's take our first steps up the ramp and on to African soil together."

"Wait a minute, we were born here! We're natives."

"Shall we be freed slaves or a chief and his wife?"

Ellen caught his mood. "How about Vasco da Gama and his wife Malindi?"

Rick played the part. "Ah, Malindi, dear, it is a pleasure to have you on this expedition to East Africa."

"And I am delighted to make the voyage with you, Mr. da Gama.

"The town we are entering, Mombasa, never had much love for me. I suppose I deserved it for acting like a pirate and looting their local dhows. But, north of here the people warmly welcomed me. I have named that town, Malindi, after you, darling."

"Vasco, dear, how romantic of you." They laughed.

In the open sheds, at the top of the ramps, bales and barrels of goods were ready to be loaded onto two waiting dhows.

"Vasco, my mood has changed. This place breaks my heart." The dock had no cranes. The loads would be carried on backs of men down the gangplank and into the holds of the dhows. Nothing had changed in hundreds, even a thousand years. "Slaves used to carry these loads, but today it is poor young men trying to make a few shillings. I feel so sorry for them."

"Your sympathy and compassion for the people here always amazes me. Ellen, I can see why you stay here."

As they walked out from the narrow streets, the massive walls of Fort Jesus towered in front of them. Yellow spotlights lit the walls. To the right of the parking lot under a white streetlight, Ellen saw the low wall. She fingered the dove necklace.

I wear it in memory of you. Melancholy thoughts whispered in her mind.

"Are those sapphires? May I see them?"

"Yes, I've wondered how much they are worth. Maybe you can tell me."

Ellen unclasped the chain and let Rick examine the necklace.

"This is a beauty. Let's go over by the streetlight so I can see it better. Very expensive! An antique and the silver work superb. Where did you get this?"

"From…my Muslim boyfriend."

"Ah, so where is he tonight?"

"He died."

"Died? When?"

"The end of November."

Rick studied the blue dove.

"You really had a Muslim boyfriend?"

"Well, we never sat down and defined our love, but he did give me this." With a teasing smile she took the necklace from Rick and clasped it around her neck.

"You will forever hold it against me for liking other girls. Are you trying to show me how it feels?"

"No."

"Where did he get the money for those fine sapphires?"

"He was a doctor."

"A doctor!" Rick smiled down at her. "I remember, a long time ago, you'd tell me stories you made up, romantic dreams. Remember, you wrote them in a journal?"

"I still make up stories." *Sad, broken dreams.* "I think by now I could write a series."

Rick laughed at her. "You dream because I'm not here to live out life with you." He took her hand. "Tonight is real." He put his strong arm around her shoulders.

They walked under the burning torches through the huge wooden doors and into Fort Jesus.

Ellen enjoyed being with Rick. He knew her well. After a laser light presentation on Fort Jesus' history, they sat at a candlelit table in the courtyard for a delicious five-course meal, ending with strong Arab coffee served in a brass pot with a pointed top.

Later that evening as they walked towards Ellen's building, Rick talked about his feelings. He rarely talked about anything deep or lasting.

"Ellen, could we be more than just friends?"

"You're a wonderful man. I like you, but as you know, you've broken my heart too many times. I have a wall guarding those emotions." *And a secret you may not like.*

"I promise I won't hurt you. I'm not young and foolish anymore."

She saw from the expression on his rough, tan face and brown eyes that he felt bad.

"What would it take to prove I'll never let you down again?"

"Time. Time to take down the wall, brick by brick, and God would have to show us it's his will."

"Yes, and we've always had different ambitions. Now, mine may be changing."

They turned off the main street. A dark green Toyota Land Cruiser drove by. Ellen's body tensed.

The driver looks like Raheem!

She turned to look again. It was too late.

No! He's not alive.

Ellen stopped.

"What's wrong? You're holding your breath."

"I...don't know."

I imagined him because we were at Fort Jesus tonight...the necklace, the peanut skins...memories made me see things that aren't there. I've done that before.

"Are you all right?" Rick asked. "Did I say something that upset you?"

"No, not at all. I just got a weird—sick wave." Ellen grabbed her stomach.

"Ellen you look like you've seen a ghost."

I did—a very scary one!

"I'm sorry," She apologized. "I'm not feeling well."

"Your apartment is just around the corner." He held her shoulder. "Should I call a taxi?"

She shook her head, no.

"It may be the rich food." Rick sympathized. "I'll take you home."

11 Good Friday Confusion

Good Friday, April 6th

Ellen didn't sleep at all. Her thoughts jumped from one problem to another. She had a team to lead. Tomorrow began a busy Easter weekend. Norm wanted their relationship to be a deeper commitment. She had to tell him the relationship was over. Rick wanted to be more than friends. Not again! *And what about the marriage license?* Being Mrs. Ashkar drenched her mind and emotions in guilt. *And who drove that green Land Cruiser?*

Raheem can't be alive. Imam Ali told me how he died. His money wouldn't be in a bank for me. I'm imagining this.

She'd prove to herself that he was not in that vehicle. She'd check out his home first thing in the morning.

At dawn she dressed in jeans and a long, deep blue Punjabi top. Raheem mentioned once how it matched her blonde hair and blue eyes. The sapphire necklace still hung around her neck.

As the sun rose, Ellen walked to the lobby of the New Palm Tree. She knew Rick was an early riser and she found him sipping coffee and reading the paper. She spoke with a soft voice. "I hoped you'd be here. Happy Good Friday."

He stood with a smile filling his face. "Thanks, and Happy Easter weekend to you too. How are you feeling?"

"Much better." *Was that a lie? I stayed awake all night.*

"You didn't have to come over here so early. You could've called me."

"I know, but I was wondering if we could finish that walk through Old Town. Let's head into some interesting alleys down by Fort Jesus."

Abdul Ashkar sat on a cement bench by the cannons at Fort Jesus talking to another man. Ellen watched him, relieved he didn't look around as she passed by with Rick.

Gold morning sun painted Old Town's moldy walls a clean yellow. Plants grew out of the cracks in old ruins.

They passed open doors. The toasty smell of frying *chapatis*, Indian flat bread, floated through the alleys along with the aroma of fresh perking coffee.

"I can see why you love this enchanted place."

Ellen pointed out historical buildings and described different architecture: Arab, Swahili, Indian and Colonial.

She eventually stopped in front of a house. "Did you ever know this family? They were friends of mine." The door was locked from the outside and the windows shuttered. A maid carried yellow water containers out of the neighbor's house. Ellen spoke to her in Swahili.

"The mama from the locked house went overseas in November," said the maid. "No one lives there now."

Ellen drew in a breath of relief. Raheem was not the man in the Land Cruiser. Yet, still on edge, she looked around. Could Uncle Abdul have followed them? What would he think if he saw her walk up to Raheem's house?

What did he learn from Norman? Will he try and get me to talk about the inheritance?

Rick's voice brought her back to the moment. "I'm considering getting out of mining and into a more settled job. Walking around Mombasa brings back good memories. I like this city."

"What would you do here?"

"Supervise the old port and dock, build cranes, and see that young men got a decent wage. Take a few dhow trips with you."

"I like that idea." She found herself warming up to him as they finished their walk.

Rick dropped Ellen off at a restaurant where the team met for breakfast. He told her he didn't want to be introduced to the group.

At the door he leaned close. "I'd like to have dinner with you at Shehnai's tonight. Can you come?"

"I love that place." She smiled. "I'll meet you at seven."

Rick set off to talk to a dhow captain he had heard about, and Ellen joined the team inside the restaurant.

"I was worried. Where did you go?" Norm motioned to a seat he had saved for her next to him.

"For a walk."

"You told us it's not proper for a young woman to walk alone. It's just not safe either. You should have asked one of us to join you."

"Norm, I've lived here all my life and know half the people on the streets. It's safer than Dallas." *Except for Abdul Ashkar,* she thought. "I did walk with a friend."

He patted her hand. "Next time tell me so I don't worry. We've waited twenty minutes for you."

He poked his knife at a piece of toast. "Why do they toast the bread then stand it up in these little racks to cool? It's hard and crusty. I like it wrapped in a warm cloth and served hot." He had taken two pieces and returned one to the toast rack.

"I think it's the British way of serving toast." Ellen reached for the discarded piece.

"What is this yellow jam? Have any of you tried it?"

Melissa smiled, the yellow jam piled high on her toast. "Norm, have you never tasted marmalade? It's made from oranges. It's tart and delicious."

Norman pulled a file out of a white cloth bag. He started to read a list of events: "Good Friday we are to meet at your patio and discuss the Easter ...."

Ellen's mind drifted.

If Raheem's alive who would know?

"Ellen, I just asked—"

His lawyer! I'll call Mr. Patel.

"Excuse me, Norm, but I have an important phone call to make."

She left her seat and stepped out the door to punch in a number on her cell phone. "Good morning, Mr. Patel. This is Ellen. I'm coming over this afternoon. I need some documents. Could you have a copy of Raheem's will and death certificate—?"

The lawyer interrupted her. "I have clients all day. You'll have to make an appointment."

"But I need to see you today."

"Please hold."

Ellen could hear two men talking.

"My secretary says she'll mail copies of the death certificate to you."

"I need them today."

Again Ellen heard two men talking. She had met the secretary. That wasn't a women's voice. "She'll send our office boy over now with what documents I can find. Where should he meet you?"

Ellen looked down the street. "At the New Palm Tree Hotel lobby."

"Fine. The boy will meet you in about half an hour." He hung up.

Why was he so abrupt? Could Abdul be making deals with Mr. Patel?

Norman stood inside the door tapping his foot and looking at his watch. The team had finished eating. Her toast remained untouched.

"Norm, take the team to my flat." She tapped the file in his hand. "They can start preparing. I'm coming in about thirty minutes."

"Where are you going? You weren't listening when I was talking."

"I have to wait for a letter. It's being hand delivered to me down the street."

"Is it that important? You're the leader of this group."

Ellen faced Norman with a sweet smile. "Norm, you are better at leading teams than I am. I'll be right back." She slipped out the door before he could argue with her.

A large manila envelope arrived nearly an hour later. She pulled out a title deed she hadn't seen before and a set of keys. On a separate note she read a scribbled apology that the office photocopier had broken down and the documents she wanted would be ready at another time. She scanned the title deed. She was the owner of a cottage near Leopard Beach Hotel.

Raheem willed me a beach cottage? Why am I just now finding out? Why is the photocopier broken? Who was Patel talking to? Abdul?

She tried to remember what Raheem had said. "I'll sell the businesses and the money will go to a bank account. The account will be in a trust for you." Nothing had been said about a cottage. She remembered Abdul owned cottages in Malindi along with some Italians. But that wasn't on the South Beach by the famous five-star Leopard Beach Hotel. Was Abdul luring her into a trap?

At her apartment she pulled Norman aside. "I received this letter." She held up the envelope. "I must respond to it today. You are doing a great job. Can you take over for the rest of the morning?"

Norman frowned. "Ellen, you can't just walk out on me. Not now."

"I'll be back after lunch."

"It's Good Friday. We can't do the program without you."

"Zillah and Mina will help you."

"But I need *your* help." Without a doubt, he sounded unhappy.

"Seriously, Norm, you've done Easter events. You're a pastor. You can do this without me."

"Not in Africa. Everything is so…hard…different here."

"It will work out. Ask Zillah. I must go. The sooner I go, the sooner I return."

She hurried out the door, down the stairway and started her VW before anyone had a chance to stop her.

12 The Dead Man's Cottage

Still Good Friday, April 6th

On the south side of Mombasa the traffic crossed to the mainland via a crowded ferry. Ellen appreciated her small VW bug as she squeezed on with vehicles just inches apart. Most drivers couldn't open their doors.

After crossing the ferry she drove south for forty-five minutes along a road lined with mango, cashew and coconut trees. The trees provided shade for little villages where a coastal people called the Digo lived. Their handmade huts had mud walls and palm-leaf thatched roofs.

Past the entrance to Leopard Beach Hotel, she spotted a gravel drive shadowed by a huge purple-pink bougainvillea bush. She turned into the narrow road. It had no sign. The trees and undergrowth crowded the edge of the gravel. Her little bug zigzagged through the tunnel of African brush.

I don't see a cottage in here! I wish I hadn't come alone.

Like popping out of a TV screen into a different world, she watched as the gravel and trees disappeared and she drove onto a well-kept lawn. Ahead, a white, two-story cottage stood, complete with little balconies running across the second floor. She parked near the back door. Red and yellow flowers bordered the house. Coral rocks enclosed their rich soil beds. The scent of sweet jasmine filled the air.

The cottage faced the Indian Ocean and paths of flat slate rock led around either side. Ellen took the one to the right.

I hope I don't meet Abdul.

She stopped and drew in her breath. A gorgeous grassy yard shaded by lush coconut trees framed the aqua sea. The sea, now at low tide, displayed layers of tan sandbanks and drew the sun's light to the blue horizon.

91

Raheem gave me this! It's beautiful!

The property was fenced. At the gate to the beach a man sat in an old wicker chair. By his uniform, she knew he must be the guard. He had not heard her car drive in.

"*Jambo*," she greeted him loudly in Swahili. He jumped and hurried to her. They greeted with a handshake. "Mr. Patel sent me. Is it okay if I go in?" She held up the keys.

"*Ndio*, yes, I was told you'd come. Welcome."

They walked back to the porch with its white pillars and arches. Black grills welded into intricate, leafy patterns filled in the archways, making the cottage secure. Through the grill she saw a huge front door made of heavy wood, carved with swirling vines and leaves and studded with brass.

"Has anyone been here?"

"Sometimes a friend of the family comes to check the place. I've heard the cottage was given to an American lady. Are you the lady?"

"Yes—I guess—yes, that's me."

He held out his hand and with a pleasant smile introduced himself.

The lock on the gate wouldn't open with the keys she held in her hand. She decided to try the back door and followed the slate walkway around the other side of the house.

A shower built of coral stone and blue tiles stood by the walkway. At its base a foot pool for washing sandy feet held fresh water. Wet footprints led down another path to a garage. A large dark mango tree filled with singing birds shaded the entrance of the garage.

Just the guard's footprints, she thought.

But looking back she saw he wore boots.

Someone's here!

"Is someone in the house?" she asked the guard, relieved he had followed her around the cottage.

"No one is here." He smiled at her.

Unlocking the back door, she entered a bright white and yellow tiled kitchen, shiny and clean—except a dirty coffee mug stood on the drain board. Next to it an empty yogurt container lay on its side.

She caught her breath.

The asthma cure Raheem mixed on the plane.

Calming herself she said aloud, "It's a family tradition and some relative left it."

The living room and dining room blended into one large area spread across the length of the cottage. Cool blues and greens with mixed accents in yellow and gold filled the room.

Blue and green, why is everything reminding me of him?

Ellen decided to look through the whole house. She opened each cupboard and went through the kitchen pantry. Someone recently stocked it with tins of baked beans, Blue Band margarine, oil and drinking water. In the refrigerator she found eggs, UHT long life milk, bread, butter and jam.

Upstairs Ellen peeked in the master bedroom. A king-size bed covered with an elaborately embroidered Indian bedspread dominated the room. A huge bay window faced the ocean. On a stand by a reclining chair a book caught Ellen's eye.

A Bible! She picked it up and skimmed through it.

A study Bible with penned-in notes. It's wrong for a Muslim to mark a holy book. Who does this belong to?

A quick flip showed no name on the front page. But a slip of paper marked where someone had read Jeremiah chapter twenty-nine. The verses were underlined.

"For I know the plans I have for you," says the Lord. "They are plans for good and not for disaster, to give you a future and a hope. In those days when you pray, I will listen. If you look for me in earnest, you will find me when you seek me. I will be found by you," says the Lord.

She found an unfinished post card tucked in the back cover.

Dear Mother,   26 March
The house will be clean and ready for you.
I miss you and am anxious for your return.
I don't eat well without your good food.
I haven't secured a job yet but have made ....

March twenty-six was ten days ago.

Is this to Raheem's mother? Is he here—alive? Ellen felt panic and alarm sweep through her body.

This is crazy! Raheem is dead! Ali told me.

93

She wiped a tear off her cheek. Confused and angry, she looked down at the Bible. The marked verse shouted at her.

> *"For I know the plans I have for you," says the Lord.*
> *"They are plans for good and not for disaster, to give*
> *you a future and a hope."*

If Raheem was alive all Ellen saw ahead for her was ruin—a divorce. Who would want her? If the secret got out that she was an Ashkar, she'd never marry. *What will my parents, friends and the kids think?*
I'm an example to the kids, and I've made such a huge mistake.

She closed the Bible. "Oh, God," she prayed aloud, "I've gone against my own beliefs. We were legally married! God please help me. Speak to me."

She turned to Psalm one-hundred and three, one of her favorite verses. Blue ink marked the chapter and a note on the side read. 'I am his number one son.'

This is Raheem's!

She placed the Bible on the stand and backed away as guilt flooded her heart.

No! Please, no! This can't be!

As she looked down at the open Bible the words called to her again. "I know, God, you are trying to speak to me, and I'm not listening."

> *"The Lord is merciful and gracious; he is slow to get angry*
> *and full of unfailing love. He will not constantly accuse*
> *us, nor remain angry forever. He has not punished us for*
> *all our sins, nor does he deal with us as we deserve."*

She stopped. "God, I've really messed up. I shouldn't have signed that marriage paper. I know it wasn't your will for me. Forgive me! Help me." She looked down at the rest of the passage.

> *"For his unfailing love toward those who fear him is as*
> *great as the height of the heavens above the earth. He*
> *has removed our rebellious acts as far away from us as*
> *the east is from the west. The Lord is like a father to his*
> *children, tender and compassionate to those who fear*

*him. For he understands how weak we are, he knows
we are only dust."*

Ellen knelt by the bay window and talked to her personal and loving God.

"Dear God, thank you for forgiving me. I yearn for your will in my life. I give you all that I am and hope to be. I give you the marriage license. I know you can work out the mess I'm in."

Finally, she sat in the soft recliner that faced the window and thumbed through the Bible. The book of Romans had the most penned in notes. Romans told how God became human, through Jesus, and removed sin so everyone could be forgiven. Clearly, the owner of this Bible had committed his life to Christ Jesus.

Ellen lost sense of time as she searched and read. Staring out at the rising tide, she recalled past conversations with God. She had pleaded with God to take away Raheem's cancer. Then she begged God to take Raheem's fear of death away and bring him into God's family.

"God, did you answer those prayers? I know you can get me out of this impossible marriage as well."

She looked out the window, her thoughts full of questions. *Raheem, are you alive? If what I read is about you, then I'm truly happy. You are one of God's number one sons. Wherever you are, I am married to you and that...that terrifies me!*

There is enormous, deep prejudice against such a marriage. Even if Raheem and I have the same beliefs, who will understand? Not his mother, or my parents, not even our friends, no one will approve of what we have done.

The post card fell to the floor. She picked it up and noticed a Dallas address written on it. Ellen recalled telling Raheem's mother about Dr. Howard.

If this Bible and post card belong to Raheem, he must be alive. But how could I inherit his money? She thought back to the day he died. *Chaplain Kilonzo, Ali, and Hatim all told me about Raheem's death. He can't be alive!*

Why did Patel give me the deed to this beach cottage?

Nothing made sense. Ellen hadn't kept track of the time. Outside the sun quietly set.

"Oh, no! I forgot," she said aloud.

"Rick," she spoke into her phone. "I can't make it tonight. I'm in South Coast and it's too late to come back alone, especially over the ferry. I didn't watch the time. I'm really sorry."

"South Coast? What are you doing there? I thought you were with the team in Old Town."

"I had an appointment here. I'm sorry."

"So, you're spending the night? Where?"

"At Leopard Beach." She didn't add the word hotel. That would be a full lie. She couldn't tell him about the cottage.

"I'll miss you. Are you sure you aren't avoiding me?"

She heard an annoyed tone in his voice. "No, Rick. I really did lose track of time. What can I do to make up?"

"Hey, I'll drive out early tomorrow. We can watch the sunrise and have breakfast together."

"An Easter weekend sunrise—you always think up the best ideas. See you tomorrow on the beach in front of the hotel. Oh, Rick, call me before you arrive. I want to be awake."

As soon as she put her phone down, it rang.

"Ellen, where are you? It's six-thirty."

"Norman, oh, I am so sorry. I'm still at my appointment."

"What kind of an appointment takes you all day?"

"I'm really sorry."

"You missed everything. Let's get together for dinner, a special Good Friday dinner."

"I think it's best for us to meet tomorrow. I'm still out of town."

"What? Where are you?"

"I'm about an hour drive from town, down at South Beach. Norman, please understand. An Indian friend, a doctor, had been very sick and I came to help out." She told another little lie. One sin leads to another.

"I'm concerned about you. I wanted to spend Good Friday with you. And, your work—this was an important day. It seems like you don't care. What's going on?"

"Nothing is going on. This came up unexpectedly. I couldn't say no. I'll see you tomorrow." Then she remembered breakfast with Rick. "I'll be late. The ferry takes a long time in the morning."

"You mean you're staying an hour drive away from Mombasa tonight? Where did you say you are?"

"I'll be fine. I'm safe at Leopard Beach. Don't worry."

"I'm new to Africa and all this puts me on edge. You drive off alone in a beat up old VW. That worries me. And then you stay away all day and—"

"I'm safe and I won't do anything unsafe. That's why I'm staying the night. I won't drive when it's dark."

She heard him sigh. "I'm still worried…I care about you."

After a long pause Ellen said, "See you tomorrow."

Norman. How will I let him know he's not for me?

She decided to go to bed early and sleep in what looked like a kid's room. She lowered and tucked in the mosquito net except for a space where she would crawl in. After turning on a table fan and turning off the lights, she crawled into bed. Two glowing green eyes spun and bounced in space, glaring at her like a ghost. She jumped out from under the net and flipped on the light. Plastic glow-in-the-dark toy spiders were attached with thread to the fan.

Some child having fun.

She cut the thread with her teeth and put the spiders in a drawer.

I'm going to dream about Raheem's ghost all night. I need to relax. I'll watch a video.

Near the bay window, in the master bedroom, an entertainment center stood with a DVD player and Hindi action movies. She called them 'shoot 'em up bang-bang movies' and every Indian family watched them. She chose the only European movie, a six-hour BBC production of *Pride and Prejudice* and placed the disc in the player.

Outside the window, the moon rose over the sea's horizon, throwing sprinkles of silver on the moving water. Wispy clouds shaped like doves peacefully glided in the night sky. Ellen leaned back in the soft recliner and fingered the chain around her neck.

Why did he give me this lovely cottage? It's totally opposite from his Swahili home in Old Town.

The Bible lay open on the stand. She turned to Jeremiah chapter twenty-nine again and placed the necklace on the page.

*"For I know the plans I have for you," says the Lord.
"They are plans for good and not for disaster, to give
you a future and a hope."*

"I believe you, Lord, and put my trust in you," she prayed aloud. "And I do the same for Raheem."

At one-thirty, Ellen woke up, the movie still playing in front of her. She had fallen asleep in the chair. Dreams about ghosts chasing doves played in her mind. She turned off the system and stretched out on the king-size bed.

Jane Austin's characters from *Pride and Prejudice* entered another dream. First Darcy's handsome face was Rick and then it was Raheem. Norman became a good sort of Wickham, and poor Elisabeth didn't fall in love with anyone because she was too frustrated.

13 Beach Boys

Saturday early morning, April 7th

Rick arrived at the hotel on his motorbike just before sunrise. He had called Ellen, waking her up a half-hour earlier. She'd slept in her jeans and the Punjabi top. She took a quick shower and was amazed to find the hot water heater turned on and new bottles of soap and shampoo.

Who set this cottage up for visitors if I am the owner? The guard said he expected me. Did Mr. Patel manage the cottage? Were those Abdul's wet footprints? Is he planning a trap? The Bible had no name, but it must be Raheem's—it had to be his. How did it get in the cottage?

Ellen ran up the beach to the hotel. She didn't see Rick. The sea lay asleep waiting for a new day in the dawn light. On the horizon an orange glow layered with pink drifted over a growing, bright yellow strip. The deep blue of the night faded into a steel gray. The sun waited to peek over the Indian Ocean.

She walked out to the water's edge and dug her toes in the cool, wet sand.

Rick came down the stone steps from Leopard Beach Hotel and quietly came out on the sand. He spoke as the sun pushed its way over the sea. "Beautiful, and just in time."

She jumped. "Don't sneak up on me."

"Sorry." He turned her to face the sea. "Watch with me." His hands slid around her waist and folded in front of her. She leaned back against his chest.

Rick, you are so romantic, but can I trust you? Will it last?

The sun rose fast and the bright heat shone on them within minutes.

"Let's walk." He took her hand. "I've looked at a house in Entebbe in Uganda. It's a big, fine-looking place on Lake Victoria. The beach there is pretty too. But, you know, I really like it here. I want to settle here. I'm quitting my work in mining."

He's arrived all the way from Congo to date and pursue me.

"The other evening I mentioned my life's ambitions are changing and I asked about being more than just friends. I know, in the past, you liked me and I let you down. I thought only of myself. Someday I hope you'll forgive me for the hurt I caused you."

"You don't have to wait for someday. I forgive you right now."

He studied her and then nodded. "Thank you. That's kind of you since you are my 'forever friend.' I want to clear the wrongs."

"Rick, how do you see God working in your life?"

"Years ago you helped me see my need for God. I know God accepted me and I him. Well…since then I've lived pretty much for myself. I want to know him more. But I'm afraid he may not want *me* anymore."

"God's spirit will never leave you, Rick."

"I know. Once we are in his family he'll never disown us—no matter what we do."

"Do you think God has planned for us to be more than friends in the future?" asked Ellen.

"I can't answer for God. He's allowed us to be very close friends. I love being with you and am hoping we will be together. But I don't want to see you hurt. I'm afraid if you knew me—everything about me—you may not like me."

As Ellen thought, she smiled to herself. *And what would* you *think if you knew I'm married to Raheem Ashkar? You'd be angry with me.*

"I understand exactly what you mean." She bit her bottom lip and nodded.

"You do?"

"Yes, I do."

"What's not to like about you, sweet Ellen?"

"I'm afraid to tell you."

"Is it that leader of the team? Is he after you?"

"Yes, he's after me, but I don't like him. That's not what you'd dislike about me." She wanted to tell him she had been married and widowed. But was she a widow? "Give me some time."

As they walked back to the hotel for breakfast a man ran up the beach toward them. He flared out his arms and yelled, "Ellen!"

She stopped with a jolt. It was Norman.

"Ellen, I've looked everywhere for you."

"How did you find me here?"

"Zillah told me how to get to Leopard Beach Hotel so I took a taxi." Norman grabbed her hand. "I'm so glad you're safe. I worried all night." He leaned in for a hug.

Rick cleared his throat.

Norman stepped back and the excitement on his face vanished. "Is this the old sick Indian?" He stared at Rick.

Rick, a tan, burly American, stood with crossed arms and muscles flexing. Norman's eyes narrowed. "Ellen, who is this?"

"Rick Davidson. He works for a mining company in Congo. He's on his way to Tanzania." She turned to her friend beside her. "Rick, this is Norman Gilberts, the leader of our team from Dallas."

Neither man spoke.

"Rick and I went to school together as kids and he wanted to see me on his way through Kenya."

"I see." She knew Norman was angry. He always gritted his teeth whenever he didn't like something.

"You didn't tell me." He grabbed Ellen's arm and pulled her up toward the bank of trees. "Excuse us," he called back to Rick.

"Do you have feelings for that…that crusty mercenary?" he whispered harshly in Ellen's face, his jaw tight.

"Norman, he's been my friend for—"

"Is he why you avoided me?"

"No, and I have not avoided you."

"I see. You came to a hotel to meet this, this hippy behind my back?"

"No, I came for the reason I told you before. Rick came here this morning."

Rick shouldered in between Norman and Ellen. Facing Norman he asked, "Hey! Mr. America, what's the problem?"

Norman stood tall and puffed his chest. "Ellen is my girlfriend. We've been together two years. And you? Why are you here?" He snorted.

"I've known Ellen *all* my life. She's my best friend. And I intend to keep it that way."

"I happen to know Ellen very well. She wouldn't choose the likes of you." Norman pulled Ellen's arm. "Ellen and I need to get back to town."

"Hey! Mr. Macho Man, tell me, if you know her so well, why am I here with her during this romantic sunrise?"

Rick and Norman fought with words, quarrelling loudly. Ellen left them and sat on a fallen palm tree up on the bank. With her head in her arms, she prayed for the confusion to end.

"Dear God, I have no peace about either of these men. I'll tell them both I'm married."

Someone slipped quietly behind her and whispered, "I've been watching you, my lovely wife."

Ellen whirled around. Raheem slipped back into the trees and down a small path into some bushes. "Raheem!" she cried. "How..." She stumbled after him.

Further up the path, he stepped out from behind a tree and grabbed her hand. "Stop yelling."

"You...you're alive!"

"Ellen." His hand trembled. "I need to give you something, but not here."

Their eyes met.

Deep excitement rattled her, then anger, fear, and panic.

Raheem, still holding Ellen's hand, said firmly. "Meet me in the parking lot at Leopard Beach Hotel. I'll wait for you."

"I can't believe it's you! I thought you were...! Everyone said..."

"Go to those men. Send them away. Then meet me in the parking lot." He turned and disappeared down the path.

Rick and Norman had stopped fighting and came running down the path calling for her.

Ellen, on her way toward them, stopped and leaned her head against a palm tree trunk, her face drained of blood.

"Ellen, you're white as a ghost," Norman said. "Were you attacked?"

"I can't believe it!" She sobbed into her hands as the reality of her situation hit her. Dread filled her. *I'm married. Married! He is alive! How did that happen? And what will become of me?*

"What's going on? Tell me." Alarm lined Norman's face. "Did someone hurt you? Are you all right?" He put his arm around her back just as Rick, on her other side, placed his arm around her. Ellen, beside herself with anguish, sank to her knees. Rick and Norman's arms intertwined around each other.

"Get your pink sweaty arm off me," Rick hissed. He shoved Norman's arm and shoulder causing him to stumble back on the path and fall.

In one swift move, Rick swooped up Ellen and carried her like a child back to the beach. "Sweet Ellen, what's happened to you?"

Norman recovered from his fall. Catching up with Rick on the sand, Ellen saw red anger steam from Norman's face. He grabbed the arm Rick had under Ellen's knees. With both hands Norman swung Rick with all his might. Ellen landed on the soft ground. Rick tripped over her and fell flat into the sand.

He jumped back up, dry sand sticking to his face and shirt. Fists clenched, he faced Norman.

Norman mimicked his stand with a brash smirk on his face.

Ellen struggled to stand and placed one hand on Rick's sandy chest, the other on Norman. "Stop!" She faced Norman. "Listen Norm, I'm your friend. For two years we dated. But we—you and I—are not going to marry. Stop this fighting!

"Rick." She turned to him. "All our lives we've been friends. We are 'forever friends,' but I'm not going to marry you, either." She looked from one to the other. "I won't marry either of you because I'm…I'm already married."

"Sure you are," Norman blurted out.

Ellen turned and stalked toward the hotel while the men followed on either side of her. "Please! I want to be left alone. Go back to Mombasa. I'll talk to you both, but not today."

Rick leaned toward her. "You're stressed."

She picked up her pace toward the hotel. The men followed her into the pool area.

"I'll call both of you when I'm ready to talk. Please? I need time alone. Just go back to town."

"I'll respect your wishes, Ellen, but I don't like it." Norman glared at Rick then turned to Ellen. "I'll see you tomorrow before the team meeting. I'm sorry about all this. I'll call you." He looked around at the hotel. "This hotel looks like a great resort. I'm sure you'll be safe here. Stay and get some rest."

"Thanks, Norm," Ellen crossed her arms.

"Mister Mercenary." Norman glared at Rick again. "Respect her request and leave." Norman said good-bye and walked to the lobby.

"That guy's an irritant." Rick reached for her shoulders but she shrugged him off.

"Could we talk tomorrow evening?"

"What about now?"

"Please, Rick, not now."

"I want to see you before that pink cowboy does. Come sit by the pool and talk."

"I need to use the restroom and I'm not coming out for a long time. Please go. I'll call you and maybe we can meet this afternoon." Ellen turned and went into the ladies' room.

Raheem is in the parking lot—waiting for me! If only I had his cell phone number. After that fight…Oh, this is awful. I can't go back to town. Now what do I do? I need to talk to Raheem. Would his lawyer, Patel, be in his office on a Saturday?

She leaned against the wall and punched in Patel's cell number again. "I know Raheem is alive. He just spoke to me. I need his cell number."

"I'm sorry. I don't give out the numbers of my clients."

"Then please call Raheem and tell him to call me. It's urgent."

She waited five minutes.

The phone rang.

"Ellen, forgive me. I acted immature." Norman pleaded with her. "I care about you and am behind you no matter what."

"Thanks, Norm. That's kind of you."

"Please talk with me—today," Norm begged. "All I can do is think about you."

"I need time alone now, but I promise I'll talk tomorrow."

"When I meet the team we'll pray especially for you. I'll lead the team today and even tomorrow if you need rest. In fact, Ellen, I enjoy leading them."

I need him off the phone. Raheem is trying to call.

"Norm, I'll talk with you face-to-face tomorrow," she insisted.

As soon as she hung up, the phone rang again.

"Your phone's been busy. I'm sitting in a comfortable chair in the lobby. Come sit with me instead of in the restroom. Or should I come break the door down?"

Ellen sighed and snapped her phone shut. She made her way to the lobby. Rick stood up to greet her.

"See, life's not so bad out here."

"Rick, let's meet tonight at Shehnai's and have dinner."

"Now that's a great idea."

"Another great idea is to let me have the day alone."

He brushed a strand of hair from her face. "Anything for you, Ellen. You're going to be all right. By tonight you'll feel fine." He circled his arms around her for a friendly hug. "I want you to be happy." Then he pulled her toward him in a full embrace.

If only I felt this sure of him all the time.

Her chin rested on his shoulder for a calm and beautiful moment.

Thick black beams above held up the lobby's thatch roof. Sisal ropes wove palm leaf thatch in even rows. Lush green plants and flowering white and pink orchids contrasted around the carved furniture. A driveway curved in and out beneath the roof. On the far side of the drive a fountain splashed and goldfish caught the sunlight. A young palm tree held a dozen weaver's nests and the bright yellow birds made a riot of noise.

Just beyond the fountain she saw a deep green Land Cruiser. Raheem stood on one foot leaning against its open door, watching her.

14 Freedom

Ellen waited for Rick to leave. He swung his leg over the leather seat of his black BSA bike. He had parked it on the hotel driveway. He tipped the guard and thundered though the parking lot toward the gate. The deep roar of the engine set off three car alarms as if fans hysterically cheered him on.

Raheem walked toward her from the Land Cruiser as she approached him.

"Ellen," he extended his hand. "Meet Lazarus."

"I'm a widow and you're dead. That is what you led me to believe, and Imam Ali did too. Why did you lie to me?"

"I am very much alive." He squeezed her hand. She pulled it away.

"It's not right. For months you've been dead. You begged me to marry you because you were dying. What am I supposed to do now? What am I supposed to feel? I cared, I trusted you. You've ruined my life." She looked into his aching green eyes.

"I didn't lie to you. I was dying. For months I didn't know if I'd live. My thoughts were confused and distressed, knowing we were married. I couldn't talk to you by phone. I had to talk face-to-face, but my body had to heal. Now I've come from overseas—I'm here to talk."

"It seems you returned over a week ago. Why did you wait to talk to me?"

"I care about you. I felt concerned about how you would react— me being alive. I also needed to settle my finances. Because I didn't die, the money you received was not given through the trust. I wanted to find out about you, too. I had heard rumors. I don't want to ruin your life. I'll do what's best for you."

"I feel violated and I'm so angry. Why did Imam Ali lie? And what about Hatim, Patel, and Kilonzo—did they know you didn't die?"

"No, Hatim and Kilonzo were told that I died. Ali lied to them and to you. I'm sorry. He didn't want us married. He was afraid you'd follow me to Dallas. Mr. Patel could not tell you without my permission and I had to see you in person first."

Ellen was still angry. "So, tell me what really happened."

"Before we talk, I have something I must show you and then give you. Can I drive you back to the cottage?"

"I guess."

Raheem opened the door and helped Ellen up into the passenger seat. The vehicle smelled fresh and new. "Is this your car?"

"Yes, you like it?"

"I like the color."

If he gave all his money to me before he died, where did he get the money to buy this beautiful vehicle? Ellen wondered.

In two minutes they arrived on the lawn by the white cottage. Raheem parked under the large, dark, mango tree by the garage.

"Wait." Raheem went around and opened Ellen's door. As she slid from the seat to the ground, he didn't move out of her way. She was aware of how close he stood and her heart refused to agree with her anger. A memory rushed over her. They were sitting on a low wall. She remembered Raheem saying, 'Things that are blue tell stories like the sea and the sky. Blue is the color of the soul, full of feeling….' Raheem was still looking in her eyes. She needed to move away from him.

"Wait," he said again, gently.

He looked up into the dark leaves of the mango tree and pointed. "Look, see there? Follow that big branch and then see a flat nest at the fork?"

"Yeah, I see it."

"That is the nest of a Fischer's Lovebird. When I was nine I made a trap and caught one."

"You came to this cottage when you were young?"

"Yes, we lived here."

But…he grew up in that Swahili home.

He went back to his story. "My dad helped me buy a big beautiful cage. I named the bird Lilly."

He looked down at her. He was so close her breathing stopped.

"I gave Lilly everything she wanted: fresh bird seed, water, even a fancy bird bath. She had a swing, and bells to ring, and a little mirror." He looked up into the tree. "I really loved that little bird, but she chirped for her friends." He stretched out his hand. "Every day I'd put my hand in her cage. Finally, she came to me and I'd scratch her neck. We were friends. Yet, she wanted to be free.

"One day I felt so badly I brought the cage to this tree and opened the door. Lilly flew straight up to her family. Each day I brought bird seed. I thought I'd never see her again. Then, one day, she landed on my hand and ate the seeds." Raheem opened his hand, large and strong. "I knew then we'd always be friends.

"Watch this." From his shirt pocket he took some seeds and scattered them on the roof of the Land Cruiser. Ellen was too short to see. "Here, step up on the running board." He lifted her on to the step. They stood side-by-side. Ellen could smell the fresh scent of soap.

Raheem whistled and a lovebird answered with a high-pitched call. He whistled again and four birds flew down to a low branch in the mango tree. "Be very still."

For a while the birds were quiet, checking out the seeds and who was near. Raheem gently tapped the roof and whistled a high-pitched sound, mimicking the lovebirds. He held out his hand with seeds in it. A flutter of green and orange-red feathers hovered near him. One-by-one, like a magical delight, they landed on his hand and on the slippery roof. They were delicate green birds with throats and chests of tomato red and soft blue tail feathers.

After they pecked and ate their fill, they flew off, twittering loudly.

"They are descendents of Lilly. I am amazed they came to me after I've been away for so long."

"They're beautiful."

"Do you like him?" Raheem asked without looking at Ellen.

"Him, who?"

"I guess that's a legitimate question. There does seem to be more than one."

"What do you mean?"

"I was told that blond preacher came to ask you to marry him. Now I see you in another man's arms."

"Who told you Norman wants to marry me?"

"I have friends."

Friends? Who had talked to Raheem about Norm wanting to marry me?

"So, are you in love?"

"No, I'm not in love with Norman."

"What about the other guy? You told me once you had a boyfriend."

"I'm not in love with anyone." She looked him in the eyes. "Honestly."

"What was that embrace in the lobby about?"

"Rick is a friend I've known since I was two. I felt upset and he was calming me."

His next words were strained. "Most men would feel great pain," he took a deep breath, "watching their wife...hold a man just as you embraced that man."

Ellen could think of nothing to say.

He is truly feeling hurt!

"Raheem—" she said softly and then stopped.

He shook his head and stepped away from the door. "Why am I asking? This doesn't concern me."

Ellen stepped down from the running board.

Raheem reached into the Land Cruiser and pulled out a faded file. "Here is your freedom: divorce papers. Everything is here. You know my lawyer, Patel. Take these papers to his office and sign them." He closed the door and walked to the driver's side. With a sad expression, he said, "I am sure you've felt anxiety since you found out I'm alive and I'm deeply sorry to be the cause of any pain."

He planned that I see these birds. Every word is rehearsed. He knows we can't be married.

As he climbed in the vehicle and closed the door, Ellen ran around to him. "Wait! Can we talk?"

"It's painful for me to talk to you."

"I have so many questions. How did you get healed from cancer?"

He turned to her. "God did it."

"Why..." *God did it! Yes, of course, he can do anything. But Raheem is saying this to me.* It wasn't the time to talk about God. "Why did you give me your cottage?"

"Please, don't ask me that."

"But, Raheem, I need to know more—about you."

"It's too hard, Ellen." He bent down and arranged something under the seat.

"Will I ever know what happened?"

"Mrs. Howard. Talk to her."

So Mrs. Howard does know Raheem. The post card was to Dallas.

Softly he said, "I'm sorry to cause you problems. The emotions I have for you—won't work. We are not meant for each other. Now, I must go." He leaned out the window. "Don't tell Asmina or Mrs. Howard that we were married. They don't know." He started the vehicle.

"Raheem, please wait."

"I don't trust myself."

"But you trusted yourself to talk about the lovebirds."

"I practiced that speech for months. Anything more I say will only hurt us."

How can I get him to stay? Oh, God, help me think.

Then she remembered. "You forgot your Bible. It's in the cottage."

He sat still for an awkward moment. "I'll get it," he said. He turned off the engine and jumped out, heading to the kitchen door.

Ellen came up behind him. "Here's the house key. The Bible is by the bay window, upstairs."

He let himself in, ran upstairs and returned with the Bible.

Ellen waited in the kitchen.

"You left this in my Bible." He opened the book. The sapphire necklace lay like a book marker in the crease. "Did you want me to take it back?"

"No." She took the necklace. "It's marking a favorite passage of—ours." Ellen spoke gently and pointed to the reference, Jeremiah twenty-nine, then read it aloud.

> "For I know the plans I have for you," says the Lord.
> "They are plans for good and not for disaster, to give
> you a future and a hope...."

"I believe that." Raheem nodded.

"I believe it, too, and I believe God has a future and hope for our friendship. Please don't walk out of my life when you've just come back into it. I thought you were dead. I need time—to sort out my thoughts and feelings."

He walked to the door and stopped. "I don't think it will help. We were never meant for each other. Emotions will get in the way and we will only hurt each other." He looked out the door. "I'm going now and we can meet some other time."

"Just one more question, please?"

He turned to her with a hard look in his eyes. "What?" He sounded angry.

"Why did you give me this cottage?"

"I came to realize I needed very few things in life." He stepped closer and grabbed her shoulders, pulling her close to him. Everything became still. Their eyes locked. His expression softened and he smiled down at her. "You look stunning in that blue Indian top." His smile left and pain filled his eyes. "What I want the most I can't have." He let her go. "I don't need or want this cottage." He walked out, climbed into the vehicle and drove away.

Ellen held the file in one hand and the necklace in the other. She tried to look though the divorce papers, but through teary eyes the forms were a blur. She wiped a tear and the silver dove, in that hand, brushed her wet cheek. She shut the file and cried.

Back in Mombasa, as Ellen parked the VW, she saw Asmina heading into her building.

"Wait! Mina, over here." She waved to her friend.

"You're back."

"What do you know about that doctor, Raheem?"

"Raheem!" Asmina's dark eyes rolled. "I just heard. He's come back to life! His mother took him to America. Now all the families with eligible girls in our community and even out of our community are trying to arrange a marriage with him. My aunt plans…Oh, well."

"We prayed for him, remember? Do you think he accepted God's forgiveness?"

"Possible, but rumor is that he's very close friends with his Imam, Ali. Another rumor is that he's engaged to someone in America."

As they climbed the stairs, Ellen thought about what Mina said. *Engaged? Did he have a girlfriend while attending college? He just told me, 'We were never meant for each other.' But he also said, 'What I want the most I can't have.' Yet he gave me divorce papers. He's so confusing!*

When she reached the door, Norman rushed to greet her. "You're back sooner than you said." His eyes searched hers. "Sorry about what happened at the beach this morning. How are you doing?"

"I'm better. Not to change the subject, but do you know what time Mrs. Howard is landing? Her flight arrives in Mombasa today."

"Zillah's just calling for a taxi. The plane lands in thirty minutes."

"Would it be all right if I went to collect her?"

"I'm sure she'd be delighted. You two are good friends. Seeing her will get your mind off all the stress."

15 Old Ladies

Saturday afternoon, April 7th

On the drive back from the airport, Ellen asked Mrs. Howard about Raheem.

"Oh, I was hoping you knew him." She smiled at Ellen. "What a nice man."

Ellen slowed the car for a group of ladies dressed in vibrantly colored wrap-a-rounds. They balanced bundles of firewood on their heads.

Ellen took another breath. "How did you first meet him?"

"An ambulance brought him from Dallas/Fort Worth Airport straight to Baylor Hospital where George works. Raheem's mother came with him. She asked specifically for my husband. I don't know where they got George's name."

"I gave them his name."

"Well, of course, why didn't I think of that? It must be my age. Yet I *did* think of you and your work here when Raheem's mother told us they were from Mombasa."

"What happened with the cancer?"

"George treated him that first day, even before preliminary tests were finished." She turned to Ellen. "It looked impossible. We were sure he would die, and we decided to pray every day for Raheem."

And I stopped praying because I thought he had died.

"God did a miracle," Mrs. Howard continued, "and kept him alive. There's not a trace of cancer in his body now. Other doctors think it's because of George's knowledge of cancer, but we know it's because of God's grace."

"Did you get to know Raheem well?"

"Oh, honey, I sure did."

Ellen hit a pothole and Mrs. Howard bounced in her seat. "Sorry."

"His mother didn't have a place to live. We asked her to stay in our guest room. Raheem's treatment took months, so we helped them find a small apartment."

"Raheem and George spent hours talking. I guess because they're both doctors. Raheem even attended church with us. That man was so thirsty to know God." She turned to Ellen with a hand on her heart. "You know, in that deep, personal way."

"Oh, God, thank you, thank you!" Ellen blinked back tears, and then smiled. "Yes. I know that way."

"It upset his mother. Sometimes I stayed home from church with her. She's a wonderful cook but…so worried for her son. She feared Raheem was losing his identity, changing his values and beliefs." Mrs. Howard frowned. "She thought he wouldn't want to return to Mombasa but he…" She glanced at Ellen, curiosity in her eyes. "You're glowing. How well do you know him?"

"As you talk, I'm getting to know him better." She raised her eyebrows. "Go on."

"Yes, and he's so handsome. Did you know he's business-minded?" Mrs. Howard didn't wait for an answer. "I own a small company and he gave me some excellent ideas. I hired him as a consultant for a short while. He told me he had owned several businesses and rental properties, but sold them because he thought he was dying. He gave all his money to a charity through a trusted friend. Amazing, isn't it?"

What would she think if I told her I'm not just that friend but his wife?

Ellen missed her street and had to drive around the block.

"He's like a son to George and me. Ellen, you said you gave him George's name. How did you get to know Raheem? You know, he never mentioned you."

"I met him on an airplane. We became friends and he told me he had cancer. I mentioned Dr. Howard's name to his mother. Did Raheem get to know Norman at church?"

"Yes, I believe they were in the same Bible study. But I don't know Norman very well. He's always with the youth. Raheem planned to return to Mombasa. I think his mother was pushing him. But I never heard what date they were coming. I'd love to visit their home."

"I'll try to find them."

How awkward for Raheem and me, husband and wife, to meet with—anyone from my church!

"I wish I had planned to stay longer in Mombasa," Mrs. Howard said as they arrived at Ellen's flat.

On an impulse late that afternoon, Ellen walked to Mama Raheem's home, praying Raheem wouldn't be there. She wanted to talk to his mother.

As she neared Mama's house she saw Imam Ali walking toward her. "Good afternoon, Ellen," he greeted her.

"I'm really angry with you, Ali. Why did you lie? Why did you phone and tell me Raheem died?"

"I did what was right. I did not want you to follow him. I found out you signed a marriage license. Musa told me. That made me upset. You're a nice person, Ellen, but you are not a Muslim. Raheem should not be married to a non-Muslim, even in a paper marriage."

A man walking by stopped. Ali greeted him with a nod.

When the man turned away, Ali continued. "When Raheem's mother told me she was taking him to a cancer specialist in the U.S., it created a perfect time to have people think Raheem had died."

"But how did...?"

"Let me finish," Ali interrupted Ellen. "I informed Musa about a good deal at a hotel north of here. He arranged the weekend there with his extended family. So, Mama's sisters were out of town on Saturday. I booked a beach cottage Saturday night near Malindi for all Raheem's friends and myself, although I didn't show up. Instead, I took Raheem and his mother to the airport, alone, that evening. Later I told everyone he had died."

Ali stopped and sighed. "I knew Raheem liked you, even loved you. I also knew he had a chance to live when the air tickets and visas to the U.S. arrived. I didn't want you talking or writing to each other. You are not meant for him. He is a Muslim and you are not. Has Raheem given you the divorce papers?"

"Yes."

"Good. I've had long talks with Raheem. He understands. Ellen, I still think of you as my friend. I hope you do not hate me for lying, but it was for your good and Raheem's."

"I don't hate you, Ali. But it was wrong for you to lie to me."

"No one likes to be deceived, but I am not sorry I was untruthful. I am sorry you are upset with me."

"Instead of being so devious, you should have talked to me about your concerns."

"Would you have listened to me? I am still concerned. Are you listening now? It is very unwise for you and Raheem to be together. Are you on your way to his home?"

"Yes, but not to see him. He does not want to see me."

Ali nodded. "Very good. You must make wise choices. Stay away from him. No one—not your friends or Raheem's—would accept you two together; neither would Allah or even who you call your God." They said good bye and Ellen walked on to Raheem's house.

Mama Raheem came to the door. "Ellen, come in, come in. You have come to see me, I hope, and not my son?"

"I came to see only you and to hear about your time in America."

"Then you are welcome."

With considerable effort, Mama moved her plump body from the heavy, carved doorposts through the wide hallway.

In the sitting room, Mama eased herself into a low chair, motioning Ellen to sit on the sofa. The sofa had big, new, American pillows on it, creating little room to sit.

"I was unhappy in Dallas. It was either too hot or too cold. And I get sick from that air-conditioning. It gives me flu. Those people, they do not live as I do. The people are friendly, but I missed my family and friends too much."

She pushed herself up off the chair. "I'll be back."

She returned in two minutes. "You will drink *chai* with me?"

"I would love some."

She disappeared again, but came back in a minute. She sat down and pulled one leg at a time up on a footstool.

"In Dallas we rented a little flat for too much money. Everything is expensive. The flat was too small. I am complaining too much." She raised her soft arms toward heaven. "I thank Allah. He spared my son's life. I thank you, too. You told me about Doctor Howard and by a miracle Raheem lives."

Ellen let her talk. It wasn't the time to tell her that Mrs. Howard wanted to see her.

"It was difficult for me. I worry. My only son changed…not so much from our family custom, but his beliefs changed. If his father were alive he would talk to him. What will become of us?" She stopped talking.

Ellen finally spoke. "When did you arrive in Mombasa?"

"I arrived three days ago; Raheem came earlier. We stayed with my sister until yesterday when Raheem was finally able to have the water and power hooked up. This place was so dusty I hired a maid. New maids never know what I want. It takes much time to train them."

With her hands she placed one leg on the floor then the other and stood. In the hall she called, "Fatima, prepare *chai*." It seemed Fatima was not around and Mama stayed out for some time.

The heavy tapestry still hung high above the sofa. Its colors of red and gold were not as bright as Ellen remembered.

Thousands of people walking around the Kaaba looking for forgiveness, and Raheem has found it.

A rush of joy filled Ellen. At the same time a deep sadness welled inside. Their cultures were completely different and societal prejudice was too deep. They were not meant for each other.

On either side of the sitting room doors hung new curtains. The breeze moved through them like a fan.

Mama Raheem returned with a tray.

"We thought Raheem's time had come. He left me with a good inheritance. I'm not poor." She handed Ellen a steaming cup of *chai* mixed with cardamom. "And of course you were blessed by what he left for your work with the children. But I must tell you, Raheem's uncle is bitter about that. He came yesterday to yell at Raheem."

She sat down. "I am proud of my son. That uncle is evil; he put a curse on Raheem. He said cancer was the curse. Yesterday he threatened Raheem, said he would put another curse so Raheem would never marry." She laughed. "Do you know how many mothers have come asking about my son?" Shaking her head she slapped her knee.

After a long sip of tea she went on. "Since Raheem's healing, and I thank Allah he still lives, he is blessed more than before his cancer. This week he went everyday to Patel's office, setting contracts, land deeds, and financial arrangements."

Every day in the lawyer's office...? Did Patel tell him I asked for the will?

"Raheem said he gave you divorce papers. Have you filed?"

"I didn't know he was alive until this morning."

"What did he say to you?"

"Not much, that's why I came to see you. I wanted to know what happened."

"Well, I have told you what happened."

A slight breeze blew the curtains.

"I am arranging a wife for him."

"Why can't his wife be...me?" Ellen asked.

"Oh, no, no, never!" Mama shook her head and stared at Ellen. "He doesn't know you. You do not know our ways."

"I have lived all my life in Old Town. I know your culture well."

"You are not a Muslim."

"A Muslim man is not required to marry a Muslim woman."

"No! It would not work. You Americans don't have enough children. I need many grandchildren to care for me. I need a daughter-in-law to cook my favorite Indian food."

She went on, "He's my only son. Many want him as a husband for their daughters. I will choose a suitable girl from the best family in our community. A Westerner like you would take him away from Mombasa, his home, my home. And what would happen to me?"

Ellen listened quietly. Mama finally paused and Ellen asked, "Is Raheem in love with someone?"

She glared at Ellen. "Have you talked with him?"

"No, I saw him this morning for the first time. Before that I thought he was dead."

She still glared at Ellen.

Ellen didn't want to argue. The conversation seemed to end and Ellen wanted to leave. "I think it's time for me to go. Let me say, before I leave, that I *do* have feelings for Raheem. He has given his life to God. I think the change you see in him is God's spirit living in him."

"I must disagree. Allah gave him a second chance and Raheem owes Allah his life. I don't see how your God has his spirit in Raheem. In Islam we are taught that God or Allah can not live in a person. He is too great."

Ellen leaned forward. "I can't limit God. He can do anything. He can even take our punishments—payment for all our sins—on himself in order to make us clean. I can't limit God in any way except that he will love us so much he'll do anything to have our love in return."

"This is the same way Raheem talks to me."

"Because it is true." Ellen softly said.

Mama didn't reply.

"I also came to tell you that Mrs. Howard is in Mombasa. She will be here only one day."

"Mrs. Howard! She and her husband were kind to us but…it worries me. They changed Raheem."

"God is the one changing him."

"It is hard for me to watch my son, his values, even his beliefs… they aren't the same. I insisted we return to Mombasa because of the Howards." She sipped a drop from the bottom of her cup. "So, she is here. Can you see the difficulty I am in? They are good people. I wish I had the same peace and love they have, but they are changing Raheem."

Ellen glanced outside, knowing she needed to end this conversation, as it seemed to be going nowhere. "I must go. It's getting dark."

"Okay, I will try to see Mrs. Howard tomorrow. I know Raheem will want to see her."

Ellen rose and took both Mamas' hands. "Thank you. Tell Raheem I'm sorry I didn't see him."

"He is never home and I am about to throw him out of the house. There is not one girl he has approved of. He says he is in love, but will not tell me who she is. He says it's not the right time to plan a marriage with this girl he loves."

"Then give him that time, and I know he will be truly happy."

A thud! A movement in one of the bedrooms, or did it come from both bedrooms?

Mama heard it too. Someone had been listening.

Ellen took the chance to leave. Mama stood up and slowly parted the curtain leading into her bedroom. Ellen called over her shoulder. "Thank you for the tea. I'll see you tomorrow."

Who is in there? Is it the maid?

But the maid stood outside chatting with the neighbor's maid.

Ellen called her over. "Have you seen Raheem?"

"He came for lunch, but I haven't seen him since. Maybe he went out."

"I heard someone in the house."

"Uncle Abdul came looking for Raheem. I watched him go in and quietly listen to your conversation. He's bad! Then he slipped into Mama's bedroom. I don't like him."

"Neither do I." Ellen walked away from the house and turned into the first alley. She didn't want Uncle Abdul to see her. *I wonder what he heard us say.*

As Ellen walked through the streets she thought of the conversation with Mama. Her questions were still unanswered.

Did Raheem have a girlfriend in America? Why do I own the cottage?

It's so dark. I told Rick I would meet him at seven-thirty.

It was seven-fifteen.

16   **Thugs**

Saturday night, April 7ᵗʰ

Ellen hurried through the narrow, dark alleys of Old Town. She kept looking around hoping to see someone she knew. Only girls with no honor or respect walked alone at night in this Muslim area.

Fort Jesus towered ahead. One more long building to pass and a small graveyard and she would be in the lit parking lot.

Over twenty years ago the long building, named Edward St. Rose, belonged to partners from Goa, India, a chemist and a medical doctor. Now it stood empty, falling apart, and condemned. Locals believed ghosts occupied it and appeared from the graveyard at night—ghosts of men who had commanded Fort Jesus.

Ahead a young man strolled toward Ellen. "Welcome to Kenya." He turned and walked beside her. "I give you a guided tour?" His T-shirt was torn and he had dirty dreadlocks.

"No, thank you." She glanced behind her. A larger man rushed up behind them.

"It is dangerous for you, out alone," whispered the man in the torn T-shirt.

"Yes, thank you, but I'm going just there." She pointed to the lit parking lot ahead. As she quickened her steps, the man behind her flung a gunny sack over her head and gripped her mouth so tight it stung. She felt the man next to her help pull the sack down over her elbows and grab her waist and arms. They pushed her into the dark doorway of the condemned building.

Fear shot through Ellen as she struggled. The sack and men held her hands tight against her sides. Once inside the door, the man behind her let go of her mouth.

Ellen thought of her cell phone in her pocket. Her hands were still free. She groped for the redial button, waited a moment and yelled, "Don't hurt me! Where are you taking me?"

"Just here," snapped the man in the T-shirt.

She shouted, "The condemned building, Edward Saint Rose, by the fort's graveyard!"

A hand smacked her face through the gunny sack. "Quiet!" the big man commanded and pushed her to the floor. As she landed something felt soft against her legs then she heard a key lock the door. The two men were in the room with her.

She heard one whisper, "Aee, what's that blue light?"

"Cell phone!"

One of the men yanked it out of her hand and tied both hands behind her back with sisal goat rope. The dusty gunny sack reeked of mold. Ellen wheezed.

God, help! I'm so scared. What will they do to me? Who did I call last and will they help me? I can't breathe!

A sharp rap hit the door and Ellen heard keys jingling and then someone enter. He pulled the bag off Ellen's head. Her eyes weren't used to the dark and she couldn't make out the man in front of her. Looking around, she tried to focus. The glint of a knife caught her eye.

The man grabbed her shoulder. "I will kill you. You, who try to convert Muslims to Christianity, you are an unclean woman and you deserve to die."

Ellen trembled. Her heart pounded. "I, I haven't converted anyone," she stammered.

The door wasn't closed all the way and as a car drove past the headlights lit the room for a few seconds. Abdul Ashkar stood before her!

Ellen wanted to scream, but her lungs couldn't breathe out more than a shallow puff.

Without a sound a white-robed man stepped in the door. He spoke to Abdul. "She has not converted anyone."

"Get out!" Ashkar yelled, livid and angry.

"Do you trust any of us in this room?" mocked the man. "Now, three of us will witness your crime."

That voice!

She turned. Raheem, dressed in a long white robe and prayer cap, looked as if he were going to evening prayers.

Raheem, you are so confusing.

"Imam Ali knows you kidnapped this woman," Raheem said. "He knows you intend to kill her. He will witness against you."

"Ali writes curses for me," Abdul sneered. "And these two men belong to me." He waved the knife at Raheem. "Imam Ali and all my friends will witness against you. You, Raheem, have rejected our religion—even your father's traditions and history."

"I am not afraid, Uncle. I have *not* rejected our history, or my father's traditions. I'm devoted to our creator, more than ever before. I have returned to take my father's place as a pillar, a strong leader in our community."

Raheem took a step closer to his Uncle. "If you are so *sure* Ali approves of this murder, then he should be here. Show him this woman and then accuse *me* before him."

Abdul hesitated. His eyes narrowed and then gleamed. "I will." He sneered. "You're merely speeding up what I planned for your fate." He spat on the floor. "You are dying because of my power."

"I am not afraid of your curses. I have a greater power. It healed my cancer."

"Ha, this power you *think* you have…" Abdul hesitated again, looking harshly at Raheem. "That power is nothing. I get what I want. I want my money, the money you gave this infidel!" He waved his knife close to Ellen's face. From his belt he drew out a small pistol and pointed it at Raheem, then toward the door. "You come with me. We will bring Imam Ali here."

"You forget he is also *my* friend." Raheem said with a steady voice.

"He will curse you for your unfaithfulness." Abdul followed Raheem out the door.

In the darkened room, the hired kidnappers sat on either side of the door, their knees bent and backs to the wall. One turned Ellen's cell phone on and off. The little blue light made ghostly shadows. They watched Ellen and whispered in eerie tones to each other in Swahili. "This building is haunted," the man in the T-shirt said. "I wish this job was over so we could get out of here."

Ellen sat cross-legged on what she now knew was a wet moldy carpet. She concentrated on her tight breathing.

Breathe in deep, count one, two, breathe out slowly. God, please save me from these men.

125

They waited in the dark.

Twenty minutes later a smashing blow exploded the dark silence. The shuttered window shattered. A machete sliced through the wood breaking the latches. The shutter swung open. "Ellen!" Rick yelled into the dark room.

"I'm here!"

The two guards shouted at the intruder as they sprang up and pulled knives from under their shirts.

Rick yelled at the men. "You kidnapped my fiancé! Now you deal with me." He broke the swinging shutter off its hinge and threw it to the ground with a loud crash. Jumping into the dark room, he slashed his machete like a sword.

Ellen ran to a corner. Rick moved toward the bigger man. "There are two men!" she wheezed a warning.

Rick swung at the bigger man's face. He ducked and Rick kicked his legs, tripping him.

The man in the T-shirt moved around Rick and lunged at him from behind. Rick twisted and lashed out at him, but too late. His knife cut into Rick's shoulder. The sound of metal hitting bone was clearly audible. Rick yelled in pain, dropped his machete and grabbed his wound. His attacker kicked Rick in the back. The bigger man landed a hard blow on Rick's head with a board from the broken shutter.

"Don't!" Ellen jumped up and positioned herself between Rick and the two men. "Don't kill him. Ashkar will be angry if you kill this man. Just tie him up."

The bigger man pushed her into the corner. "Shut up, woman."

Rick passed out from the blow to his head.

They kicked Rick again as they tied his hands and feet with more goat rope. Cursing in anger they rolled him onto the carpet. Ellen moved next to him on the floor and could see he was breathing. Her own breath came in quick gasps.

At the broken window a shadow beckoned to one of the kidnappers.

"Where is Abdul?" Ellen heard the tall thug demand. She couldn't hear what the man whispered in reply.

The man turned to his friend in the T-shirt. "I told you Imam Ali wouldn't come."

"What do we do?"

The man outside the window replied, "You both stay here and wait for Abdul. He's coming just now."

Then the man climbed in through the backlit window. He stood over Ellen. In the dark she saw a wall of white robe in front of her. He bent closer to her face.

"Raheem!" she gasped.

"Did I hear this man say he is your fiancé?" He pointed to Rick. "Or does he lie?" She felt his hot breath on her face.

"He lies. I'm married to you." Ellen whispered. Her voice shook in fear.

Raheem stood up and faced the kidnappers. "Untie that scum who loves her. Abdul wants only the woman. I will take him."

The taller man sneered. "We heard what Abdul said to you. We're not doing anything until we hear from him. Just sit down and shut up."

"My uncle will be here any minute," Raheem sounded angry.

He looked out the broken window while pacing in front of it. After a moment his cell phone rang. "Hello, Uncle. I told you I would wait for you. I'm here." Raheem turned quiet for only a moment. "Talk to them yourself."

He handed the phone to the tall thug. "It's for you." The taller one snatched the phone and listened. Immediately he grabbed his partner and said in a low voice, "Police are coming. Run!" The kidnappers scrambled for the open window but Raheem blocked them. "The cell phones," he demanded. Two cell phones were thrown at him as they climbed out the window and disappeared down a dark alley.

Raheem bent over Ellen. "Thank you, God!" He gently tried to untie her hands. "Sounds like an asthma attack. Can you walk fast?" She heard concern in his voice.

"I'll try," she said in short breaths.

The knot around her hands was bound too tight. He gripped a knife from under his robe.

Rick moaned and turned his wounded body. As he gained consciousness, he saw the knife in Raheem's hand. "Leave one scratch on her and I'll kill you!" he hissed.

Raheem looked at Rick. "Easy, big man, I'm on your side. Listen to me. Don't cause any problems and we'll get out of this."

"Why did they run?" Ellen asked.

"Not now." Raheem worked quickly on the cords around Rick. "We've got to get out of here, fast. You, fiancé, can you stand?" Rick raised his good arm and Raheem helped him up.

The door was still locked and the thugs had taken the key.

Raheem grabbed Ellen's arm as well, helping her, then Rick out the window. He hurried them down the street toward Ellen's flat.

Away from the building Raheem walked silently, holding Ellen's hand. She wheezed short and shallow gasps. He stopped twice allowing her to catch her breath. Rick followed, moaning in pain as blood dripped from his shirt.

"Where is your uncle?" Ellen asked between breaths.

He looked around. "I hope he's still writing curses with Ali. Ali locked me in a room alone while he went to talk with Uncle. Just as he closed the door he pointed to a key behind the door. As I ran back to you I called Naushad and asked him to mimic Uncle Abdul telling the thugs to run because the police were near. I thank God it worked."

At the gate of Ellen's building, Raheem whispered, "Don't go out alone, my dear one. Abdul will be in a rage." From his pocket he took her cell phone. "Stay inside. Rescuing you isn't easy." As he handed her the phone he took her hand. "Ellen, go back to Dallas with the team. You're in danger here. Fill out the divorce papers before you go and then forget me." He looked sadly into her eyes.

Ellen's heart turned over.

How can I forget you?

Raheem turned away and walked into the night.

17 Ticket to the USA

Night, April 7th

"He is married—to you? That Arab?" Rick bent over in pain.

Ellen watched Raheem walk away.

He has feelings, yet he walks away. It's useless. Nothing will work between us. She sighed.

"He's an Indian, not an Arab." She turned to Rick. Blood oozed from his wet shirt and dripped on the step. "You're seriously wounded. You need help!"

Rick's knees buckled and he sank to the ground.

Ellen rushed out into the street. Raheem was several buildings away. A *tuk-tuk* drove past her. She shouted to it. "Stop!" The driver slammed on the brakes. "See that man in the long white *kanzu*. Bring him here. He's a doctor. Look, my friend has fainted." The *tuk-tuk* revved its little engine and sped forward.

Ellen's lungs ached. She knelt by Rick and saw that he was unconscious again. Air squeezed in and out of her throat in small hisses. Her fingers were blue. The stress was bringing on a serious asthma attack.

In minutes, Raheem returned. Tearing the hem from his robe, he bound Rick's bleeding wound.

With the help of the *tuk-tuk* driver the two men lifted Rick onto the back seat.

"Ellen, there's a taxi. Flag it down."

"I feel like fainting. I can't breathe," she wheezed.

Raheem whistled and stopped the taxi then turned to Ellen. He took her hand and rubbed the back of it. "Try to slow down. You can make it. Breathe in, hold it, and now push it out. There, keep that rhythm and you'll have plenty of oxygen."

129

He opened the taxi's door. "Try to be calm. In five minutes I'll have an inhaler for you." As Ellen got in, he rolled down the window to give her more air. Raheem told the taxi driver to take her to Mombasa Hospital. He returned to the *tuk-tuk* and crowded in with Rick who lay sprawled on the seat.

At the hospital Raheem helped wheel Rick into the emergency room. Ellen sat on a wooden bench outside the swinging doors. Her ribs hurt. She wheezed in tight gasps.

Raheem returned with a small box. From it he took an inhaler and shook it. "Here, two puffs." In less than a minute, Ellen's breathing returned to normal.

"Thanks."

"I think you're all right now." He turned and disappeared through the doors.

Fifteen minutes later he returned and spoke matter-of-factly to Ellen. "Rick has regained consciousness. He has been stitched up and is getting a little blood. The emergency doctor wants him to stay a day or two."

"I'm sure he fussed about that."

Raheem sat on the bench next to her. His voice softened, "Just so you know, the hospital hired me. My first day is tomorrow."

"Congratulations."

"Dr. Langat interviewed me. I was impressed when he prayed with me. I'll be following him around, getting to know the place. So I'll check on Rick tomorrow. I'm sure you'll come visit him?"

"Yes." She was aware of his eyes taking in her blue Punjabi top, then the sapphire necklace and finally his eyes met hers. The halls around them stood still as their hearts churned. "Yes, I'll come."

Sunday, early Easter morning, April 8th

At five-thirty on Easter morning, Ellen, Melissa and Darla sat on the chairs in the corner of the roof patio. Ellen's Easter tradition was to watch the sunrise and thank God for forgiving her sin. The girls had spent the night in Ellen's flat, keeping her company and helping her to feel safe after the kidnapping. Melissa and Ellen had stayed up late talking.

A long Easter program was planned for the team and the kids. Ellen decided to check on Rick early, before seven. While at the hospital, she'd find out when the doctors were coming on duty and return again at that time to visit Rick.

Blood transfusions, stitches and pain tablets had done their healing on Rick. But the drain tube in the deep wound looked ugly. His arm hung in a sling.

"Hi, Rick."

"You look pretty."

"It's my Easter outfit." She wore a cool green Punjabi suit.

Rick rubbed his bearded cheekbone. "Last night I tried to rescue you, and a proud Arab in a white dress walked us away from danger."

"He's an Indian."

"So, tell me what happened. My head is fuzzy from the pain pills."

Ellen tactfully changed the subject away from Raheem.

"Rick, you called me your fiancé last night. Why do you want to marry me?"

He smiled and held out his hand. "You're a tough girl. You can live the kind of life I am into." He put his hand on hers. "And you're pretty."

"Tell me more."

"You'd be loyal to me."

"Loyal when you wink at girls who think you're so wonderful and tough?"

"Oh, come on."

"Rick, I want to marry a man who loves me so much he will give his life for me."

"Didn't I just do that?" He touched his sling. "I'll always have a scar to remind me of the time I came to rescue you."

"That Indian man risked his life too."

"I'm trying to remember...what did he say before I passed out?" Frowning, he rubbed his forehead.

"I am married to him."

"I don't believe it." He smiled shaking his head no. "Plus, you wouldn't marry a..." He stopped shaking his head and the smile turned to a frown. "Am I remembering something you said? A doctor gave you the sapphires. So...you're not making this up. Is this what you thought I'd dislike you for—being married? I think I *will* get upset. What's going on?"

"Let me explain. I met him—well, we met and he had cancer. I thought he had died right here in this ward."

She told Rick about Uncle Abdul's greed and Raheem's money and how she signed the marriage license just before he died. She explained about seeing him in the Land Cruiser the night Rick took her out and how it had upset her. At Leopard Beach Hotel, he had waited for her in the parking lot and she had needed Rick and Norman to leave.

"He gave me divorce papers, my freedom." She hesitated, wondering if she should go on.

"Have you filed?"

"Not yet."

"What are you waiting for?"

"I..."

"You can't love him."

Ellen lowered her eyes.

"He's a Muslim. You can't stay married to him."

"I think he's accepted Jesus."

"Dressed in that Muslim white robe and prayer cap—he was part of the group that kidnapped you."

She turned and faced him. "We're all going to wear white robes in heaven. Until then it's his culture and it's the same culture as mine. I've lived in Mombasa as long as he has." She smoothed her Punjabi dress. "He is also as much of an American as I am. We both spent eight years in the States."

"You're dazzled, infatuated, by someone with a handsome face, a doctor, a rich man. Where are the divorce papers? I'll help you fill in the blanks."

"Rick, you *are* my best friend. I thank you for caring for me. I am grateful you tried to rescue me last night." Ellen moved her chair closer to his bed.

"That's my girl. Now, let's talk about us. Come to Uganda and get away from Mombasa. It's dangerous here."

"Rick, you and I don't work for the same purpose. You've loved Georgia, Barbara and Marita. I'm not like them. I work in a city with children. You need a woman with high energy who loves adventure, wide open space. Someone..."

Melissa entered the door. "Hi, Ellen. Hey, Samurai." She wore a flirty smile. "I've brought flowers." She moved the bedside table out from the wall and placed the flowers on it. "Look, I arranged them around a machete. Thought you might want a weapon on hand in case the thugs return."

Rick smiled, amused.

"Ellen and I stayed up late and talked about you."

"She would have lots of stories." Rick laughed.

"So many—I just had to meet you. She says you're sailing on a dhow to Dar es Salaam. I would absolutely die to do that."

"Then join me and persuade Ellen to come."

"What's the doctor said about your wound?"

"I haven't seen him yet."

Ellen got up and let Melissa sit.

He's looking at Melissa in that dreamy way I know so well. There's a good match, or at least a distraction. Melissa is in Africa for the adventure.

Ellen walked toward the door. "Let me go ask when the doctor is expected."

She returned a few minutes later. "He'll be here at two-thirty. Melissa, let's come back then. We need to help with the Easter program this morning."

As they walked back to the flat Melissa prodded Ellen with questions. "I'd love to sail on a dhow. Would it be difficult to change my airline ticket?" Ellen offered all the information she could, especially about Rick.

It was eight o'clock and Norman had just arrived when they walked in. "Hey, Ellen, are you all right?" He walked out to the hanging garden. "I want to hear about last night."

Ellen told him the basic story, leaving out details—like Abdul Ashkar's name and referring to Raheem as 'just a friend.'

"I want to hear about the beach, too. I feel bad about what happened. You were so upset."

"Let me tell you that story another time. Right now the team is waiting to go to breakfast with you." Ellen pointed her chin at the group.

"Yeah, you said something about being married."

"I'll have to explain that. Let's talk when we have time. Do you mind if I don't join you for breakfast?"

"Yes, I mind, but I understand after what you've been through."

Ellen needed time to sort her thoughts. She sat alone in the far corner of her patio.

What does Raheem think?

She tried to remember what Raheem had said. 'The emotions I have for you won't work. We are not meant for each other.' 'Return to the States with the team. Go back to Dallas. Forget you met me.' His mother would arrange a marriage soon. Ellen needed to sign the divorce papers.

'What I want most I can't have,' he had said.

He loves me. Last night on the hospital bench he looked at me with those yearning eyes.

Was he lying to her? The things he did and said didn't make sense. He contradicted himself.

I must stop these strong feelings I have for him. We're not made for each other. It'll be easier to forget Raheem in the U.S. And being away until Abdul cools down is wise.

Half an hour later, Mrs. Howard arrived and sat beside Ellen.

"I regret that I planned only two days here. Tomorrow I fly to Tanzania to visit a hospital there."

"I wish you were staying longer, too."

Norman came and joined them. "Ellen was assaulted twice yesterday." He spoke to Mrs. Howard, "once on the beach and then in Old Town last night. She must come back to the U.S with us. Persuade Ellen she can't live here alone."

Ellen responded with words that surprised even her. "Norman, I agree with you. I'll go back to the States. I'll book an airplane ticket Monday morning."

18   **A Couple**

Easter afternoon, April 8th

"How's the big wound feeling?" Ellen and Melissa heard Dr. Langat ask Rick as they walked into the hospital room. Raheem stood next to the doctor. He greeted the girls with a handshake.

As the doctors examined the wound, Melissa turned away to survey the hospital room. Ellen sat on the extra bed watching Raheem.

The hospital provided a bed for family, a quiet air-conditioner, mosquito net, fan, a refrigerator, TV and DVD machine. Melissa looked behind long curtains that were pulled across a glass door. Beyond, a wide balcony overlooked the Indian Ocean. "This is beautiful. Who'd have thought Kenya had hospitals like this?"

"It's less than fifty dollars a day," Ellen informed her.

"I'd hospitalize myself just to rest and relax."

"I've heard people do that." She wanted to add, *I'd be admitted just to be near Doctor Raheem.*

Ellen! You are leaving for the U.S. in order to forget him.

Rick interrupted her wild thoughts as he looked curiously at Raheem. "Ellen, is this guy...?"

She bit her lower lip. "He's an expert on sapphires."

"Is he the guy with more than one life?" Rick asked, still focused on Raheem.

"Actually," Raheem smiled confidently down at Rick, "I'm the guy with a *new* life."

Dr. Langat, who had not been listening to the conversation, finished his exam. "Rick, you're a strong man. You'll heal quickly. Your wound needs to drain a bit more. We'll have you out of here tomorrow. Now, I have a procedure I practice with my patients. May I pray for you?"

"Yes, of course."

"May I say the words?" Raheem asked.

"Go right ahead."

"Our great God, I thank you for making Rick a strong man. Thanks for his bravery last night. Please heal him quickly and I ask that this wound leaves very little scar. In Jesus' name, I pray, amen."

The doctors left the room together without further words.

"I'm impressed," Melissa said with wide eyes. "Praying for patients, wow! Ellen, you seem to know that good-looking doctor. I'm jealous!"

Rick turned to Melissa. "In most Indian communities, the mother finds a girl for her son. I'll bet his mother has a long procession at her door. You wouldn't want to wait in that line."

"I'll bet he marries only the woman he loves," Ellen said.

Rick looked at her with a knowing nod. "Or is he married to her already?"

"If he is married to her, and if that woman is God's number one choice for him, then I'll be...a very happy woman." Ellen sat on Rick's bed.

"I believe you have made the right choice." Rick touched her hand. "Go for it, Ellen. I couldn't approve of a better man or match."

Ellen was caught by surprise. "What...when did you change your mind?"

"What are you guys talking about?" Melissa moved closer. "I'm confused."

"After you explained it to me this morning, Ellen, I realized that I'm just your big bro', your protector. You've told me many times that God hasn't called us to the same work. You belong here, not in Congo or Uganda." Rick sat up straight in the hospital bed. "You and the doctor love caring for people, you're both Mombasa natives, you both love God, you love each—"

Someone coughed at the door—they turned. Raheem walked in with the medical chart and placed it in a file box on the wall.

"We've been talking about you," Rick volunteered.

"I know. While filling out this chart by the door I heard every word."

No one spoke.

Raheem broke the silence, a bright smile on his face. "I need something from Ellen."

"What's that?" Rick caught Ellen's eye.

"Time."

"Time?" Rick smiled. "You're a good man, Doc. But don't take too much time."

"Thanks." Raheem moved across the room and whispered something to Ellen then left.

Melissa shook her head. "I am so confused."

"What did he say, Ellen?" Rick sounded determined to know. "Out with it."

Ellen's face flushed. "He said, 'Return to the States for your safety. Be patient for God's will.'"

She didn't tell Rick all that Raheem had whispered to her. He had said, 'It's not the right time for the woman I love to plan a marriage, nor is it the right time for me. Go back to the States for your safety. Wait for God's will. I'll send you word when the right time comes.'

Ellen remembered her conversation with Mama. She had told Mama to give Raheem the time he needed, waiting for the girl he loved. Mama must have discussed that conversation with him.

Wednesday night, April 11th

Three days later Ellen sat by Norman on the airplane. "I'm so excited!" he beamed. "You by my side, flying home after twelve hard days. I never dreamed it'd be so hard. I don't think I slept through one night. Back to my own bed and a shower with water pressure. And most of all you're with me."

He thinks I'm all his. At the beach I was serious and he didn't get it. I'm about to break his heart!

"Norm, you've spent twelve days at my home. What are your impressions?"

He sat up and changed his tone. "Old Town is fascinating, like living in history. I love the sixteenth century."

"Would you go back? Could you make it your life and work?"

"No, it's not my kind of place. I've loved being in Mombasa, but I belong in the U.S."

"Listen," Ellen faced him. "I'm saying this from my heart. You and I are not on the same life path. I know God wants me to live and work in Mombasa. I love it. It's my life. Can you understand that? God wants you to work in a church in the U.S. He is not leading us together."

"You can't say that. You can't live in that difficult place alone."

"I've lived in Old Town since my birth."

"The main reason I came—our friendship—it's more than just friends. I'm in love and need to know you're committed to our relationship."

"Norm, I know." She studied her nails. "You're in love with a girl who went to college with you, but it's not who I am now. I can't give you a commitment."

"Have you prayed about this? Do you think God wants you alone in that city where you're in constant danger?" With a tender voice he added, "I'm sure he'll reveal to you what he's saying to me."

"God has shown me through my gifts, my desires, and circumstances that he wants me in Mombasa."

"Then why are you on your way to Dallas?"

"Norm, you're making this hard. You know I need a break. That doesn't mean I'm quitting."

"Are you in love with Rick?"

"No." She smiled. "If I were I'd have married him long ago. No, I don't love him."

"Zillah hinted that a guy in Mombasa likes you."

"She's right." Ellen nodded without looking at Norman.

"Did I meet him?"

While she thought of what to say Norman asked, "Would you marry him?"

"I can't marry him. I'm already…"

Ellen touched the sapphire necklace that Raheem had given to her to remember him when he was gone. Since that day at the cottage she hadn't removed it. With no plan or direction for a future relationship with Raheem, she wore the dove as a token of hope. How could this hope be growing stronger when she was flying to the other side of the world? Ellen changed the subject.

"I don't have that spark, Norm. I can't feel for you what's not there."

Norman took a deep breath. "I care for you more than any girl. Ellen, I can't imagine another girl like you."

"I know a girl who loves you with all her heart and I'm not talking about me. God wants her to be a pastor's wife. I think you should meet her."

He shook his head. "No, I don't want to meet..."

"She's a close friend of yours."

Norman stared at her, shocked and confused. He finally said, "Not that I want to start something, but now I'm curious."

"I'll tell you about her, but first I need to go—back there." Ellen motioned to the back of the plane. A few seats back sat Tim and Darla. Melissa had stayed in Kenya for another week.

Ellen approached Darla. "May I switch seats with you? It's time you talked with Norman and told him everything."

Sunday evening service, April 22nd

Ellen sat alone near the center of the big American church, one seat from the aisle. She had hoped a friend, anyone, would sit in the seat by her. No one did.

For the past week she had stayed with her parents. They were away this weekend for a friend's funeral.

She had talked with Norman twice, telling him they'd always be friends, but that their relationship was only that. She left him heart-broken. The empty seat next to her seemed to be his place, so no one sat by her.

She touched the dove necklace. *Two more weeks and I'll be back in Mombasa.*

Ellen's mind wandered from the message.

Mombasa, was it really home? In the U.S. she felt safe. Women could walk freely, shop, jog in the park, and be themselves. Windows and doors had no iron bars. Yards weren't walled in and no hired guards stood at each gate.

Plastic bags didn't blow in trees and cover the ground. Everything stayed clean with dishwashers, car washers, cemented walks and mani-cured yards. Cars, homes, public buildings were air-conditioned with no electric failures. Water flowed down the drain effortlessly and no one reused it to flush toilets.

I could live here, although the comforts seem artificial. What would I do? The meaning of my life, what would it be?

Ellen thought about the kids in Mombasa and how she lived to help them. In the U.S., what would she do beside increase her comforts? She knew her place. She belonged in Mombasa.

Thoughts of Raheem kept interrupting her. She knew he had accepted God's way of forgiveness. Her heart felt a strong tug for him. He had feelings for her, too. Would they ever talk about them? They were still married on paper. The necklace was still around her neck. What would happen to their relationship, to these emotions? How would this end? Dreams of him kept invading her concentration.

The preacher brought the message to a close. "Let us have a time of commitment and reflection. You're invited to come forward and pray or you may pray where you stand."

People came and knelt at the stage steps.

Ellen prayed silently.

"Dear, God, I give all I am and hope to be to you. I know you want me in Mombasa. I need help, Lord, with my emotions. What do I do about Raheem? You've always been faithful to me...."

Someone slipped into the seat next to her.

She didn't open her eyes. She kept praying silently.

"God, take Raheem out of my life if—"

A familiar voice tenderly said, "Ellen."

She jumped.

"Shhh," He motioned with a finger to his lips.

"How did...? What are you...?"

"Shhh," he whispered. "I'll tell you later."

Ellen's heart began to pound.

This is my wildest dream. Ellen, wake up.

A mischievous smile crept across Raheem's face. His arm circled her shoulders. "Follow me." He stepped into the aisle with her in his grasp.

"Where...what?" she protested.

He leaned near her ear. "I'm walking you down the aisle."

In a daze, Ellen walked with Raheem. "We're in church. Be serious. Don't joke."

"I am serious."

When they reached the front, he faced her. "Will you pray with me?" They knelt. With his arm still around her shoulder he prayed in a low whisper, "Oh, God, we need your wisdom. Guide us. We need to know about a forever love relationship. Show us even today."

Ellen watched him as they knelt. His green eyes radiated joy and excitement.

Ellen's face glowed.

This can't be real!

The eyes that invade my dreams, my daydreams, and my random thoughts, this man who cares about people, who's given his life to heal people, he's kneeling with me before God and a church full of people. He is praying for us!

"Breathe, Ellen. I don't think you're having an asthma attack."

"I can't. You've taken my breath away!"

"I love you," he whispered.

"This is the happiest moment in time. I couldn't—" She stopped.

"Couldn't what?" asked Raheem.

"Sign those papers."

The invitation ended. They got up and sat on the end of an empty front row, his arm on hers, comfortable and strong. The speaker dismissed the congregation.

Dr. Howard rushed up and greeted them. "Raheem, you're back in the States so soon?"

Raheem smiled and raised an eyebrow communicating unspoken words. "I have business that calls me here."

"How long are you here?"

"Two weeks." Ellen heard Raheem answer as Norman began speaking to her from her other side.

"I see Raheem knows you."

"Yes, quite well."

Norman frowned. "I know him quite well, too. We were in several Bible studies together."

"Do you like him?"

"Sure, who wouldn't? Why did he have his arm around you?"

"I guess because we're married."

"Married?" Norman blinked.

Ellen waited, letting the news sink in. "Remember at the beach, I told you and Rick that I was married?"

"You were exaggerating, trying to get us to leave you alone." Norman shook his head. He searched her face. "It's true?"

Ellen nodded.

"But Raheem lived here in Dallas." The frown deepened between his eyes. "Why didn't you tell me?"

"I thought he had died—that I was a widow. Then at Leopard Beach, remember how upset I was? He was there. He flew back to Mombasa…he gave me divorce papers." She paused. "But we love each other—it's a long story."

"When did you marry?"

"About five months ago, on his death bed. Only he didn't die. I think you know more about his healing than I do."

"Ellen—*you*—married to Raheem!" Norm shook his head. "But he never mentioned you."

"How could he when he was supposed to be dead?" said Ellen. *And Norm, you talked to everyone about marrying me!*

"He's the man for me, Norm." She turned and looked over at Raheem. Their eyes met in that magnetic clinch. He wasn't paying attention to Mrs. Howard who gushed over him. He motioned Ellen to join him. Norman followed.

Raheem stood tall and wrapped his arm around Ellen. "Dr. and Mrs. Howard, and Norman," he cleared his throat, "I want you to be the first to know that God is confirming to Ellen and me…" he smiled down at her, "an arrangement we made a while ago." He didn't explain.

"Congratulations." The Howards hugged Raheem and Ellen with pleasure and approval.

Norman sat down in an empty seat. Leaning forward, his chin in his palm and elbow on his knee, he stared at the floor.

Darla walked up. "Hey, Ellen, what's the occasion? You're beaming."

"Darla, do you know Raheem?"

"Yeah, he went to a study Norman led."

"Well, we are…a couple."

"You two—together? That's perfect."

Ellen whispered to Darla, "Look at Norm. I think…"

Norman sat deep in thought.

"He'll be okay, you know," Darla assured Ellen, "he's been talking with me." Ellen saw a sparkle in her eye. "He knows you aren't for him, but I guess seeing you as a 'couple' with another man hurts."

More friends approached. Raheem chatted with Tim about medical school, while Ellen talked with Melissa who had just returned from

Africa. Melissa and Rick were emailing everyday. Ellen asked her to write Rick a message saying, "The doctor is in the U.S. with Ellen."

Melissa had not sailed on the dhow with Rick. Rick had been told to give his wound six weeks to heal. He was staying with a friend in Nairobi.

"Well." Melissa laughed. "Since I couldn't sail on the dhow maybe I'll join the Marines in the Indian Ocean and guard ships from Somali pirates."

Raheem and Ellen were the last ones to leave the sanctuary. It was lit in soft light.

"Ellen, sit with me a minute. What better place to talk than in a place of worship to God."

19   The Clasp

In His sitting room

Seated on the top steps of the sanctuary's stage, their knees nearly touched. Raheem spoke of his deep commitment to God. "I've accepted God's forgiveness and I know he loves me."

"Raheem, that fills me with joy greater than any I know. When I visited your cottage and went through your Bible, God showed me that you loved him."

"It's not my cottage, it's yours. You asked why I gave it to you." He took her hands, holding them on his knee. "When you asked for my death certificate that day on the phone, I was at Patel's office. I had gone over the finances and I saw you were given the bank account. The cottage was part of the will, too, but I hadn't died. I still wanted you to have it—so you'd think of me."

"Think of you! I thought of you constantly. Your memory haunted me."

"I didn't mean to leave my Bible, but I think God planned that."

"Your Bible amazed me. Through it God spoke to me about you." Her blue eyes widened and danced with feeling. She wanted to tell him the whole story.

"He makes the best matches." Raheem took Ellen's arm and placed it over his.

"Perfect matches," she agreed.

"By the way, my mother chose a girl for me."

"So, you disagreed with her, she kicked you out of the house, and now you are homeless."

"No." He laughed. "Try again."

"I can't guess."

"She chose the perfect one—you."

"Really? She made it clear that never, ever would she consider me your suitable wife. And she presented me with many reasons."

"I overheard that conversation. Remember my mom getting up to serve tea? She was checking on me. I pretended to be asleep in my room. She didn't want me listening. Sorry for snooping, but I will always remember you asking my mom, 'Why can't that wife be me?' I was thunderstruck. You constantly kept your distance from me. Then you informed her. 'I have feelings for Raheem.' I almost spun off the bed. And when you said, 'Give him that time and I'm sure he'll be happy.' I did fall off the bed."

"I thought I heard something."

"Mom found Uncle Abdul listening from *her* bedroom and she got so angry she threatened to move to the States and become an American. That sly crook! I followed him when he followed you. He phoned his thugs and I heard their plan to kill you. I prayed so hard. And then God miraculously helped us walk out of that dark Edward Saint Rose building."

"What has happened to Uncle Abdul?"

"Ali and I are best friends and Ali knew about Uncle Abdul's drug deals, illegal money, bribery, and much more. I asked Ali to help me. Uncle Abdul assumed Ali was on his side because of curses he paid Ali to write for him. What a shock Abdul had when Ali wrote a curse against him for threatening you. In fact, Ali told him to leave Mombasa or be cursed again. Uncle Abdul moved to Malindi."

"Ali doesn't want us together. He talked to me about how wrong it was."

"He spent hours telling me the same thing. I told him I gave you divorce papers. He thinks we're getting a divorce."

"That night your white robe and prayer cap confused me."

"I figured if I looked like I was going to prayers I'd have the approval of the general public, if I needed them. I especially wanted Ali on my side. He was very upset about the marriage license. He may still be a problem for us."

"When did your mom change her mind about me?"

"I told her what Uncle Abdul did to you. She became alarmed and disturbed because she really does like you.

"I began talking to her about you and she realized I had feelings for you all along. We discussed you—a lot." Raheem brushed a hair from the side of Ellen's face. "She likes you except for one thing—you're not a Muslim. She also realized I am able to make my own decision. I told her I needed you more than any girl she could find. Finally, she couldn't think of a girl in our community who suited me more than you."

They still sat on the top steps of the stage, his hand over hers, and Ellen became aware of how close his face was to hers. His eyes looked into her heart with deep radiating admiration.

"The day you left she told me she had chosen you, Ellen. I told her it was too late, you had flown to the States. She called a taxi and we headed for the airport. But all the flights were full. The first seat I could get didn't arrive in Dallas until this morning. I've come straight from the airport."

"Yes, you have a way of appearing unexpectedly. You told me you would send word when the right time came and instead you've come all this way in person."

"I am the word in person. The right time is now." He placed his hand on Ellen's Bible. "Jesus is the Word of God. He came in person, at the right time to give himself…even so far as to die for those he loved. I want to love you like God loves me.

"My heart, my mind—all of me wants to stay with you." He looked tenderly into her eyes. "Ellen, live by my side as my wife, my lover, and my companion." He lightly brushed his fingers on her arm. "If you can't, then I promise never to…appear to you again."

"Raheem, I have such strong feelings for you. I've cherished you from that first flight. I've fought my feelings—fought my thoughts of affection for you. I would tell myself, 'Don't look at him,' because of reasons, big and important. Then…now, God changed everything. I'm free to love you—and I do deep in my heart."

"Let's stay married—stay together." He spoke in a quiet tone. "Ellen, may I see the necklace? I want to show you something."

She unfastened it.

He pointed out tiny letters on the silver clasp that Ellen had not noticed before, the words 'my love.' Raheem looped one end of the chain around Ellen's ring finger and held the dove on the other end to his heart. "Dove, it rhymes with…my love."

Ellen tipped her head and looked up at Raheem. "Does this mean we're engaged?"

"Yes, we're finally engaged after being married for five months."

Ellen laughed sweetly. "That's even hard for me to believe."

He clasped the chain around her neck and then with both hands holding hers he stood, pulling her up next to him.

"Tomorrow I'd like to go on our first date."

"And where will that be?"

"How about we go to a shop that specializes in diamonds?"

Ellen and Raheem walked hand-in-hand to the back of the church.

"Are we doing this backwards?"

"Maybe, but I *did* marry the girl I love."

Dear Reader,

It's my prayer that you take a moment and consider your relationship with God.

Do you know, for sure, that God has accepted you as his adopted child? Is your answer A or B?

A. I am not sure what God thinks of me.
B. I have assurance that God has accepted me into his family because I have accepted and believe Jesus died for my sins and God has forgiven me.

Can you talk to God, on a personal level, and hear him talking to you through his Word?

A. I do not hear God speak to me.
B. I love to hear God speak to me from his Word and I am committed to read it everyday because of my love for him.

If your answers are A, would you like to learn more about how much God loves you? He wants you to accept a gift, the gift of forgiveness of your sin and eternal life with him. In the Word, God's Book, in Romans 3:23-25b it says:

"For everyone has sinned; we all fall short of God's glorious standard. Yet God, with undeserved kindness, declares that we are righteous. He did this through Christ Jesus when he freed us from the penalty for our sins.

For God presented Jesus as the sacrifice for sin. People are made right with God when they believe that Jesus sacrificed his life, shedding his blood."

Jesus paid the penalty for your sins. Then he didn't stay dead.

In Acts 3:24, in the Word, it says: "But God released him from the horrors of death and raised him back to life, for death could not keep him in its grip."

Jesus is alive! Can you tell him you believe that and accept it?

If you do, he gives you another gift, his Spirit. Jesus wants to live in you through his Holy Spirit.

In Islam, the five daily prayers have a line that has people pray, 'show us the right path.' The Book says "Jesus told him, "I am the way, the truth, and the life." John 14:6.

J.R.P. Morse
invaded.dreams@gmail.com

Author's Note

All the characters in this story are created from my imagination. My prayer is that through Raheem and Ellen my readers will see truth. God helps us work out relationships when we first accept his truth. The relationship we can have with creator God is offered to all people. Anyone can be his number-one son or his number-one daughter. That adoption brings true joy and peace.

I do not advocate marriages between Muslims and Christians. They are customarily filled with pain and conflict.

The places named in my story were real places in Mombasa when I wrote the novel, except the train station burnt down some years back—a tragic historical loss.

My goal is to tell people about God's forgiveness and about the friendship he wants.

I live in a big traditional 'Arab' house with my spouse and children.

J. R. P. Morse
invaded.dreams@gmail.com